CAPITOL CRIMES
THE BEST OF
CAPITOL CRIMES MYSTERY

CAPITOL CRIMES CHAPTER OF

SISTERS IN CRIME

EDITED BY KATHLEEN L. ASAY AND PATRICIA E. CANTERBURY

THE BEST OF CAPITOL CRIMES
Copyright 2013
Edited by Kathleen L. Asay and Patricia E. Canterbury

Foreword
Copyright 2013 by Peggy Dulle
T-Bone
Copyright 2013 by Kathleen L. Asay
Bubbles' Baubles
Copyright 2013 by Elaine Faber
The Bridesmaid Wore a Bullet
Copyright 2013 by M. J. Georgia
A Simple Question
Copyright 2013 by Eve Ireland
Corpse Pose
Copyright 2013 by R. Franklin James
Among Strangers
Copyright 2013 by Teresa Leigh Judd
Murder, Self-Taught
Copyright 2013 by Virginia Kidd

The Dream
Copyright 2013 by Nan Mahon
Guilty As Sin
Copyright 2013 by Denise Martin
Stiffed
Copyright 2013 by Joyce Mason
Murder Interrupted Me
Copyright 2013 by Patricia L. Morin
Bad News is Good News
Copyright 2013 by Karen A. Phillips
Delta Suicide
Copyright 2013 by J. A. Pieper
The Case of the Caramelized Corpse
Copyright 2013 by Cindy Sample
Death Valley Redux
Copyright 2013 by Linda Townsdin

Cover Design by Karen Phillips, PhillipsCovers.com
Formatted by IRONHORSE Formatting

ISBN: 1492932744
ISBN-13: 978-1492932741

CONTENTS

FOREWORD
BY PEGGY DULLE

Capitol Crimes has done it again!

In 2008, the Sacramento chapter of Sisters in Crime put out an anthology of short fiction by our members: *Capital Crimes, 15 tales by Sacramento Area Authors*. Published by Umbach Consulting, it enjoyed steady sales and good reviews.

Now here is our second anthology, *Capitol Crimes, the Best of Capitol Crimes Mystery,* another fabulous collection of stories by our talented authors. Some names will be recognizable in the Sacramento area, but for others, this is their first publishing credit, although I think you will have a hard time guessing which ones! Every story has a local setting, including local sights and businesses. In some, the Sacramento connection is central and in some it's peripheral, but it's there in all of them. There is something for everyone in this eclectic collection of stories.

If you are looking for murder and mayhem – it's here.
If you are looking for intrigue and suspense – we have it for you.
And if you are looking for a story where the bad guy loses and the good guy wins – we've got that, too!

Capitol Crimes has been the Sacramento chapter of Sisters in Crime for almost twenty years. Sisters in Crime is an international organization with thousands of members and chapters world-wide. It offers a network for advice and support to women mystery writers. Members (both men and women) include not only authors, but publishers, agents, booksellers, librarians, and readers. We welcome all who love a good mystery – to write and to read!

Capitol Crimes meets monthly (except July and August) on the third Saturday of the month at Rancho Cordova Library. For more information about our meetings and membership, please check out our website: www.CapitolCrimes.org.

Enjoy!

PEGGY DULLE is President of Capitol Crimes, the Sacramento Chapter of Sisters in Crime. A prolific writer, she has published three mystery series under Peggy Dulle (www.PeggyDulle.com). As PD Musso (www.PDMusso.com), she also writes a science fiction series and a fantasy series.

T-BONE
KATHLEEN L. ASAY

In high school, Tom Nelson had loved fast cars, football and pretty girls. He drove a souped-up, flame-painted Chevy, was captain of the football team the year our school had its best season in twelve and could have dated any girl he wanted, even me. Though I married my best friend's brother, Jim, a few years later, it was not until my senior year that I even looked at him. I'd been too besotted with Tom Nelson. And while I would happily stay on in my hometown, everyone knew Tom expected to ride through the future as he had through high school, with the wind on his face and the game ball in his hand—a long way from the apartment above his parents' convenience store in downtown Sacramento.

It ought to have come as a surprise to him then, though no one really knows, that his body was not as indomitable as his character. At 80 miles an hour, as clocked by a city cop who saw the whole thing, Tom's body was only as strong as the sheltering metal around it. And that metal was only as good as the mind behind the wheel. Did he see the other car too late, or did he simply assume he could outrun it? In the last seconds before certain impact, he swerved, avoiding the collision and likely sparing the other driver's life, but Tom had nowhere to go and his speed was too great. The Chevy flew over the curb at the corner in front of Rosy's Diner, straight into the base of the restaurant's twenty-foot signpost. A perfect t-bone, the cop told me later.

I was in Rosy's that day, nearly thirty years ago. It was a school hangout and though we'd all graduated a few days earlier, we'd had yet to find another place to go. We sat and talked idly about graduation, our plans for the summer and college, how glad we were to be moving on, and our voices were overly loud as though volume could make up for uncertainty.

Tom was late, which may have been why so many of us were still there after we'd finished our lunches. It was two fifteen *in the afternoon*. Not the early hours of the morning. It was June, the sun not only shining but hot. I'd had two large glasses of lemonade, but they were not enough to quench my thirst. I sat in a booth next to a Sutter Street window squinting at the shiny pavement of the parking lot and the blinding reflections from car windows, those parked and those rolling past on Sutter and Q Streets.

Tom's Chevy approached on Q and I think my mind registered his speed before the other car appeared on Sutter, brakes squealing. Then the Chevy turned sharply and piled into the signpost. Inside the restaurant, the sound of the crash was deafening, and people began to scream. But even as the noise was building, I was scrambling out of my booth and headed toward the door. I opened the door cautiously, but Tom's beast of a car came no further.

I inched forward, peering into the crush of metal and broken glass. No Tom. Relief washed over me for an unguarded moment so I was doubly shocked when I found him. He'd been thrown from the car and lay broken and unmoving in the gutter beside the restaurant's driveway. He wore the white shirt and black pants he'd had on for graduation, though he'd chucked the tie and there was blood on the shirt. There was blood everywhere around and on him. His thick brown hair, so nicely combed for the ceremony, was dark and shiny wet with it. Before I could get closer, a police officer yelled at me to stay back, and soon a fire department ambulance pulled up next to Tom and three uniformed men rushed to his aid.

As though I'd been preparing for that moment my entire life, I reached into my purse and pulled out a notebook and pen. I'd use larger notebooks in later years, but all I needed was a blank page, and I had several. I checked my watch and wrote down the time, the date, the name. June 16. Tom Nelson. I wrote down what I'd seen from inside and what I was seeing at that moment. I spoke with the shaken driver of the other car. Then I turned around and talked with the kids coming out of Rosy's. I was still working the scene when a reporter from *The Sacramentan* showed up and began asking questions. By then, most of the witnesses had left. Tom had been loaded into the ambulance and hurried away. A tow truck had arrived for what was left of his car. There was only me and a couple of cops.

I made a deal. I would tell the reporter what I had seen if he would read my story after I wrote it and tell me what he thought.

He agreed. He even gave the story to his editor. Eventually, the paper hired me as an intern and a few years later I was a reporter.

Three days after graduating from high school, Tom also entered the second phase of his life, a life far different from anything he'd ever imagined, a life he might not have chosen to live if he'd been given the option. But he was 17, and his parents made the decision for him. His friends from high school, the football players, the pretty girls, visited when they got the chance, stumbling over things to say until they cried and awkwardly backed out the door to return to lives that had not been cut short, that progressed as they were supposed to, and most never returned.

Tom's parents took their departure philosophically. After all, what could either side gain from the visits? Tom, a skeleton of his former self, sat propped up in a wheelchair making only random eye contact, and wasn't that only by chance? He could speak, but what he said made no sense. It was just noise. As for his visitors, what could be more awkward than conversing with that ruined shell and telling it about the game-winning TD you'd scored or the internship you'd been offered with the Governor's office? I thought of his parents sitting in the next room, their profuse gratitude for the visit, their regrets for their son. They insisted the visits pleased Tom, but how could they tell? I certainly couldn't.

I went occasionally. And while I never got closer to Tom than I had been in high school, I felt quite friendly with his mother. I doubted Tom knew who I was, but I didn't know if my life would be what it was if he hadn't ruined his so spectacularly.

One afternoon more recently, I stared across my desk at a summer intern who had a story she wanted to pursue without telling me what it was about. On a hot day in early August when news was short and tempers were, too, she'd been late back from lunch because she'd been tracking her subject.

"*Tracking?*" I repeated. I asked her to close the office door. She did and settled into a guest chair with an air of impatience and crossed her legs so she could swing the one on top. She was short, small-boned and pixyish except for a prominent nose, her "nose for news," she'd told us before anyone else could pin it on her.

"You know," she said. "I need to get... him alone, so I can ask him some questions."

"What questions?"

She shook her head. "I'm not going to tell you, Mrs. Cane. You'll just take my story and give it to someone else. It's my story. And it's big.

You'll be glad. No one else knows it."

I closed my eyes, not high on patience myself, and cringed. "That's not the way it works at a newspaper, Lyndsey. If you come up with an idea for a story, you bring it to your editor. Me. For all you know, someone else might already be working it."

Her face had wrinkled while I was talking. Distress? No, anger. She rose fluidly to her full five-foot-three and tossed her short cap of ginger hair. Her voice was icy.

"Nobody else is working this story. I told you, it's mine. If you don't want it, I'll take it somewhere else. Lots of places would take a story like this. It's *news*, unlike some of the stuff this paper prints."

Oh, the glory of being twenty-something. I'd been working for the paper her entire life. What did I know?

Only that I'd been much like her, once.

She had her hand on the door and was about to walk out with her self-sufficiency intact.

"Lyndsey," I said, "think hard about this. If you go after this story alone, your summer here is finished."

She shrugged and did not look back.

Jim and I were clearing the dishes from a late dinner that night when the paper's crime reporter called. "I'm at Constellation Restaurant on J," he said. "Do you know it? Senator Dominguez, Sheila Anne Dominguez of Marysville, has been shot. She's still alive, but it was a close one. The odd thing is that one of our interns was here, too. She was injured— someone thought she might have stepped in front of the senator—and was kidnapped."

"*Kidnapped*?"

Jim raised an eyebrow at me and I gave him one back.

"The shooter took her with him," Nick said.

"Lyndsey." Before Nick could agree, I said, "I'll be there. Fifteen minutes."

Though the last glow of sunset had faded from the sky, the day's heat lingered. Porch lights revealed couples conversing on doorsteps; headlights lit up dogs being walked. I thought I knew where Constellation was, but if I hadn't, the flashing lights of official vehicles would have told me. I drove to the next block and found parking. Then it was only a short hike back to where cops had the sidewalk blocked off and were discouraging both the press and public.

My mind had raced through what it knew about Sheila Anne Dominquez from Marysville, a state senator from a farming and bedroom community north of Sacramento. Married and trading on her married name to appeal to her constituents. She'd been in the Assembly one term, was in her third year in the Senate. Liberal. Ambitious. A scrapper, a headline seeker. Was she Lyndsey's subject? Talk about being in over her head, Dominguez would eat her alive.

I found Nick on the sidewalk just beyond the parking lot for the restaurant. He had little more to tell me. The restaurant host had called him to say one victim was Dominguez. She was a regular, often ate late. One of her aides was with her so it was a working dinner. He hadn't known the young woman with the red hair. She'd come in and gone straight to Dominguez, and he'd heard her say, Lyndsey something from *The Sacramentan*. Her questions started an argument. The host tried to get her to leave, but then a man came in, dressed in black and wearing a ski mask. He found the senator, pointed a gun at her and fired. But as he did, the young woman screamed and threw herself in front of Dominguez. Angry, the man grabbed the young woman by the arm and took her with him out the front door.

"Short and quick," Nick observed.

"The cops say anything yet?"

"Nada. I gather they're still talking to the other patrons and the staff."

"She can't have been too badly hurt."

"The senator?"

"No, Lyndsey. I don't give a crap about Dominguez."

The front door of the restaurant opened and a tall, gray-haired man in a suit emerged along with the police spokesman. They conferred briefly with a uniformed officer then came directly to Nick and me. We'd all met before so there were no niceties. The tall man was O'Connor, a detective sergeant.

"Your reporter was talking with Dominguez," he said. "She on a story?"

I hesitated but couldn't lie. "Not officially."

"*Unofficially?*"

"No. I don't know what she was doing."

"Well, looks like she saved the senator's life. We'll need her particulars. You can tell Frank here."

"We heard she was kidnapped."

"That's what we heard, too. We'll be looking for her, you can bet on it." He tossed his head toward the uniformed man he'd spoken with before. "We're looking for witnesses on the block, and we'll get it out to the city. They won't get far."

With that, he walked away leaving Frank to get what we could tell him about our intern. I did what I could, full name, address, phone numbers, a photo. When we tried to ask questions of our own, we got nothing. Nick growled as Frank thanked us and departed for other game, followed by what was by then an impatient herd of reporters. As customers began to exit the restaurant, Nick hurried to snag quotes ahead of the pack.

I turned around and scanned the block from the restaurant door to as far as I could see in any direction. Business lights had gone out, but occasional second floor apartments still glowed and residents watched us from between curtains.

Bright letters above a store across the street spelled out, Nelson's Market; a smaller sign in the window said, Closed, though the interior was still dimly lit.

Upstairs, in the apartment, lights blazed. A yellow glow from inside cast shadows around the seated figure on the balcony.

"Wait a minute," I said. "O'Connor!" He turned reluctantly. "Tom Nelson's still up. Maybe he saw something."

"Old Tom? Poor bugger could see through walls and not be able to tell anyone about it."

"No," I found myself arguing though I didn't know if I even believed it myself, "I think he can tell. You just have to *listen*. Though maybe he'd rather talk to me than to you." I smiled. O'Connor looked at me like I was crazy. "It's worth a try," I added.

He made the same scan of the block that I had, seeing the darkening doors and windows. "Aw, hell," he said, "I'll never live this down."

O'Connor walked quickly like he was anxious to get his embarrassment over with. I told him to stand back when we reached the building and to be quiet while I spoke through the intercom to Tom's mother who was reluctant to invite me in at that hour. Once inside and in the apartment over the store, I put my hand to my mouth to tell him to be quiet and left him in the front room while I went out onto the balcony alone.

"Hi, Tom," I said. "It's Liz."

"Ho," Tom said, which his mother had long decreed was his version of "Hello." "Ho, ho, ho." I thought Tom also used the sound when he was happy or he wanted to agree with something the other person had said.

His face had lost its sharp angles over the years and was bland, as if thought and emotion never reached it anymore. I suddenly felt stupid. Of course, he couldn't tell us anything. He hadn't for years. Still, I leaned against the balcony railing so he could see me, too, as he faced the restaurant and the flashing lights.

"Do you see the lights, Tom?" I asked. "That's the police out there."

There was a shooting in the restaurant a while ago. Did you see a man run out? He was pulling a woman with him, a pretty woman with red hair."

Tom stared down at the street. He made a noise, hummed. No tune, just a note of music.

"Ho."

I touched his hand on the arm of his chair. His hand lay like something dead. "Yes," I said encouragingly.

More humming. He wasn't paying attention to me at all. He never had. Not even in high school.

"Tee. Tee." Sounds without meaning. I heard heavy footsteps, O'Connor coming.

"Tee. Bone."

I waved O'Connor back.

"T-bone?" I said to Tom who repeated the sound several times. He did not look up.

I repeated it to myself. Had I heard him correctly? T-bone? Like a steak? Or like his accident? But I was the only one who heard the cop that day.

It was nonsense. I looked where Tom was looking. "Constellation" glowed in electric blue letters on a black wall above the cool white light of the restaurant's entrance. In the distance, a brightly lit corner of the Capitol dome, in front, cops and a growing number of reporters and the curious waited for something to happen.

Hopeless.

Then I saw it: Lyndsey's candy apple red vintage Thunderbird among the everyday cars in the small parking lot beside the restaurant.

"T-bird?" I said. "T-bird?"

More humming. Then, "Ho. Ho."

"That's Lyndsey's T-bird." I spoke clearly so O'Connor would understand and hear the dread, the urgency I felt. "She met Johnny Zaharis at a Thunderbird car club. We told her he was dangerous, and she said she'd broken it off, but— A reporter's been looking into a connection between the Zaharis gang and Dominguez. Maybe Lyndsey found it.

" Those older Birds are special, aren't they?" I said to Tom. "Did they drive off in one? Is that what happened?"

I heard heavy footsteps again, going out this time. Too slow. *Hurry*, I wanted to shout. The street door banged. Tom's head jerked upward at the noise, then fell.

"Ho," he said to the lights and voices below.

O'Connor, as though he had heard my fear, emerged at a trot, shouting orders.

I was offered lemonade and a seat on a sofa while I waited, but I preferred the small metal chair beside Tom on the balcony. He hummed and once in a while said, "T-bone," or something like it. The sound of the night, meaningless, or the answer to my question? I had no idea. Time dragged while I thought about the Zaharis brothers and what punishment they'd inflict on Lyndsey.

O'Connor didn't come back, he called.

"Zaharis had her," he said when I answered. "They'd done a favor for the senator, and she'd promised more in return than she delivered. Your girl went to warn her they were after her, but Dominguez denied the whole thing. Then the girl saved her life. Ironic."

"Thanks," I said. "Is she okay? Lyndsey?"

"More frightened than injured. She said to tell you, you were right." He snorted. "I'll admit you were right about old Tom."

"I'll tell him."

But when I looked at Tom again, his eyes were on me as though he'd never seen me before. Did they brighten? Or was that only the light reflected from the street?

I bent over with the intention of kissing his forehead in thanks but instead touched my lips to his. I went home and told my husband I had finally kissed Tom Nelson.

I did not say that Tom had kissed me back.

Ho!

KATHLEEN L. ASAY is a long time member of Sisters in Crime and a past president of Capitol Crimes. A writer and editor, she has written for arts magazines and volunteer organizations in several states. In 2009, she had a story in and edited *Capital Crimes*, the chapter's first anthology of members' short fiction. Her first novel, *Flint House*, featuring journalist Liz Cane, was published recently by Bridle Path Press. Learn more at www.KathleenLAsay.com.

BUBBLES' BAUBLES
ELAINE FABER

He stood in the dark hallway. A thrill of anticipation plunged down his spine. Sixty-two, sixty-three... until he reached one hundred. Every detail carefully planned. Kill her with the flashlight, run down the back stairs, drive quickly to the motel and pretend disbelief when he heard of his wife's most unfortunate demise.

He opened Myrtle's bedroom door, rushed across the room, swung the flashlight, and struck her temple. Myrtle's blood splashed across the sheets and pooled on the pillow beneath her head. He stood over her as the crimson liquid bubbled and oozed down her wrinkled cheek and dripped over the edge of the bed to the floor, drip... drip... drip... .

Herbert stifled a yawn and forced open his eyes. His bedroom furniture took on a ghostly appearance in the breaking dawn. His stomach seized as the memory of Myrtle's blood-soaked head filled his mind. *My God, this time I really did it. I killed her! I need to get out of here before—*

"Herbert! Herbert! Can't you hear me? I'm calling you."

His heart plummeted. He sat up and rubbed his eyes. Fingers of cold sweat crept along the small of his back at the sound of her voice.

"I need to go to the bathroom. Come and help me."

Still alive! He sighed and staggered from his warm bed. When would he have the courage to kill her? He stumbled to his wife's room and threw back the covers.

Too late. She lay in a puddle of wet sheets.

"Now, look what *you* made me do," she snapped. "Why can't you come when I call? Bring me dry clothes and run my bath. You can change the sheets while I bathe."

Myrtle shrieked when Bubbles jumped on the bed. "And get that damn cat off my bed!"

Herbert shooed Bubbles off the bed and helped Myrtle pull off her wet gown. Flabby layers of fat bulged beneath her sagging breasts. Blotchy skin on her skinny legs reminded him of chicken legs draining on the kitchen counter. He shuddered.

"I'll run your bath, all right," he muttered while he filled the tub. "Then maybe I'll hold your ugly head under the water until you turn blue. Who can say you didn't slip in the tub?" The corner of his mouth twisted in a smirk.

"Meow."

Herbert turned. Bubbles waddled through the bathroom door.

"Hey, Bubbles." Herbert buried his face in the cat's long dark fur. He drew a ragged breath and swallowed the lump in his throat. "If it wasn't for you— I can't go on like this much longer."

The cat wiggled from his grasp. Herbert sighed and went back to Myrtle's room to help her into the tub.

While Myrtle napped later that morning, Herbert drove to the Pet Club. First, he placed bags of Kitty Friskies and kitty litter into his basket, then he pushed his cart down the aisle until he came to the display of animal collars. He glanced up and down the aisle. No one was watching. Just what he needed: a pink cat collar with rows of clear rhinestones.

Perspiration beaded his brow as he hurried through the checkout stand and home with his purchases.

Along the way, he had a firm talk with himself. This time, he wouldn't chicken out. This time, he'd go through with the plan. While Myrtle slept, he'd open the safe and remove the diamonds she'd inherited from her father. Some months ago, he'd seen her hide the combination to the safe between the pages of D.H. Lawrence's erotic novel, *Lady Chatterley's Lover*. *Lady Chatterley's Lover*, indeed! Now wasn't that a joke?

How many times had they quarreled about those damn diamonds? How many times had he begged her to sell them? How many times had she refused? He was just a slave, that's what he was, but not for long. This time he'd do it.

At last! She slept. He slipped past her bed, pulled the book from the shelf and retrieved the combination. Then he turned the dials, opened the safe and grabbed the envelope of diamonds. He tiptoed to the kitchen and, with jeweler's pliers, removed the rhinestones from the cat collar, replaced them with Myrtle's diamonds and clamped down the prongs.

A perfect fit.

He placed the exact number of rhinestones into the envelope and popped it back into the safe. Still asleep! He spun the dial then slipped the paper with the combination into the book and restored the book to the shelf.

"Here, Bubbles. Here, kitty, kitty." He fastened the collar filled with diamonds around her neck. "There now, my Beauty, isn't that pretty?"

Herbert grinned as Bubbles licked at the foreign object and ran into the living room.

Next, he looked up the number of a motel in downtown Sacramento and made reservations for Friday night.

"Herbert! Herbert."

His blood ran cold. His stomach roiled. Oh, how he hated her. "Myrtle!"

"Bring me another cup of coffee. Why don't you heat my coffee in the microwave? You know it's only lukewarm from the coffeepot. If I've told you once, I've told you a hundred times— You're just worthless."

He slipped the rat poison into Myrtle's coffee. It swirled in a series of delightful designs as it sank through the amber liquid and settled in a pool in the bottom of the cup. He crept up the stairs. "Here's your coffee, sweetheart. Drink it all down like a good girl."

Myrtle drank and within a minute, her face grew deathly pale and she writhed in pain. Her skinny fingers clutched at her throat as she gagged, shuddered and died in hideous agony. He stood over her body as the blood trickled from her twisted mouth and dripped onto the floor, drip... drip... drip... .

"Herbert? Did you hear me? I'm waiting!"

Herbert jerked. Back from his reverie, he poured the coffee, placed it in the microwave and set the dial for two minutes. Maybe she'd burn her ugly mouth when she drank it.

What fun it had been to imagine new ways to commit murder. But now he'd settled on a plan and put it into motion. He smiled as he carried the coffee up the stairs.

When she fell asleep that night, he slipped out the door, eased the car from the garage and drove to the neighborhood pub where he engaged in conversation with the local drunk, Chuck. After three beers and several trips to the boy's room within half an hour, the neon lights spelling *Beer and Wine* began to slither across the bar's dark window. He blinked to bring the letters into focus. Now, he'd pretend to be drunk. Not much effort at all, and he made a convincing argument.

"I could have me a little book store but, no, the old lady won't sell her blasted diamonds. What good are they locked up in the safe?" He put his hand over his eyes and peeked through his fingers. Would Chuck buy the act? Indeed, he looked quite interested.

"In the safe, ya say?" Chuck tossed back his drink. "Yer right, diamonds don't do nobody much good there in the library safe."

"Nah, not in the library." Herbert picked up his beer. "Safe's in the bedroom, behind the picture over the stereo, that's where she keeps them." He sighed. "And she doesn't even trust me with the combination. She tried to hide it from me. But I figured it out, alright. 36-24-36. Now, who does she think she's kidding?"

Herbert slid his gaze toward the bartender, making sure he'd remember their conversation. Chuck would be the perfect fall-guy for Myrtle's murder.

Herbert choked back a sob. "I'm going to leave her, that's what I'm going to do. Friday night, right after she goes to sleep... at eight o'clock." *Maybe a little over the top? Nah!*

Chuck nodded, his face the picture of sorrow. "Friday night, ya say? Here, pal, have yerself another drink. You'll feel better."

Herbert drove away from the bar, satisfied with his performance and in no hurry to get home.

He tiptoed up the stairs to where she lay sleeping. His fingers twitched as he reached for her scrawny neck. He clutched her throat and squeezed until his fingers ached and her face turned a ripe shade of purple. She gasped. Her thrashing knocked her water glass from the nightstand. At last, she lay still. He stood over her body as water flowed across the nightstand and dripped onto the floor, drip... drip... drip... .

"Herbert? Is that you? Where have you been? You've been gone for over an hour. I'm lying here in pain, as if you cared. Bring me my medicine. And be quick about it."

Myrtle! Still awake.

Herbert no sooner entered her bedroom, than Bubbles jumped on the bed and pushed her head under his hand. He stroked her back, pausing for a moment as his fingers passed over the diamonds on the collar. Not long now. "Come on, Bubbles. Myrtle needs her pain medicine."

On Friday afternoon, Herbert sat in the library, his heart pounding, reading a magazine. He glanced at his watch. 3:00. Any minute now, she'd be yowling for her coffee—

"Herbert! Bring me some coffee. You know I like my afternoon coffee. If you weren't so lazy, you'd bring me a cup before I had to ask, but you don't care if I lie up here and die of thirst, do you?"

He stood and grinned at Bubbles. *Time to get the show on the road.*

He carried his packed suitcase into Myrtle's room.

"Where do you think you're going?" She scooted up against the headboard, needing no assistance. Odd, as she had required help every morning for the past three months.

"I'm leaving you." Herbert smirked. "Get yourself another coffee boy. I've had enough."

"You can't leave." Myrtle's eyes grew wide. "Who will take care of me?"

"In the words of Clark Gable, 'I don't give a flying fig.'" Herbert turned toward the door.

"That's not what he said, you fool," Myrtle called after him. "He said, 'frankly my dear, I don't give a damn.'"

"And frankly, my dear, neither do I." Herbert hurried into the hallway where he turned to wink at Bubbles. "Don't worry. I'll see you real soon." He scampered down the stairs grinning like a schoolboy just let out of school. "Bye-bye!"

Herbert drove to a busy shopping center in Rancho Cordova where he paid cash for a thin pair of gloves and a large flashlight, then on to the Starlight Motel, a block from the Crest Theater. He registered, paid with a credit card and asked for the receipt. "Can you tell me where I could find the nearest movie house?" His face was the picture of innocence.

The clerk handed Herbert a printout from the Crest Theater. "They're playing Hitchcock movies at the Crest all month. Just down the street. Tonight's movie is, *The Birds*."

He'd seen *The Birds* a dozen times and knew the story line well. He'd read about the Hitchcock movies in *The Sacramento Bee*. "Sounds like fun. Thanks for the information." He went out the door, waving the brochure.

At 8:00, he drove to the theater, bought a ticket and found a seat in a dark corner. At 8:50, he left his coat and hat in the seat and stole out the back door, leaving it slightly ajar. He hurried back to his South Sacramento neighborhood, stopped on the next block in front of a dark house, tiptoed through their backyard and climbed the fence into his own yard. He crept across the patio and used a screwdriver to break the lock on the back door. *This time I'm doing it!* His mouth felt as dry as a cardboard hatbox.

He glanced at his watch: 9:20. She should be asleep. It was so clear, how he'd do it, just as he'd imagined a hundred times. *He tiptoed across the room toward the lump in the bed and swung the flashlight down onto her forehead. He heard the crunch as the bones of her forehead gave way beneath the blow. He stood over her body as the blood poured from her temple, down her ugly cheek and then dripped from the edge of the bed onto the floor, drip… drip… drip… .*

Open the safe, take the envelope with the rhinestones and sneak back into the movie house. He should arrive about the time the birds attacked the Bodega Bay residents. After the movie, he'd speak to the motel clerk and tell him all about it. Between the credit card receipts, the movie ticket and the motel clerk's story, he'd have the perfect alibi for her estimated time of death.

Tomorrow, he would pretend he'd lost his key and ask his neighbor to bring over the spare. They would discover the tragedy together. Chuck would be arrested for Myrtle's murder and the theft of the diamonds. Before long, Herbert would file a claim for Myrtle's life insurance and for the stolen diamonds. In six months, he'd be rich.

Satisfied with his plan, Herbert crept up the stairs and stood outside her bedroom door, his heart pounding so loud he was sure he'd wake her, the flashlight clutched in his sweaty hand. He put his ear to the door and listened. His forehead prickled with moisture.

Silence.

She's asleep. This time I'll do it for sure! He reached a shaking hand toward the door handle, turned it then charged into the room, the flashlight raised.

Bubbles lay sprawled across Myrtle's pillow.

The picture over the stereo drooped at a 45 degree angle.

The door of the safe hung askew. He crossed the room and peeked inside.

Empty except for an envelope with his name scrawled across the front.

He dropped the flashlight on the bed, ripped open the envelope and held the letter in the beam of light.

Dear Herbert:

I'm tired of pretending I'm an invalid. You are such a fool. Look how long you waited on me hand and foot! You aren't going to leave me, I'm leaving you. With Daddy's diamonds, I can live like a queen. Good-bye, sucker. Myrtle

Herbert stared at Myrtle's empty bed. Bubbles stretched and the light from the flashlight glinted off her collar, casting a rainbow of colors across the far wall.

She's gone. I'm free!

Herbert laughed until tears rolled down his cheeks. No more fetching coffee. No more changing wet sheets. No more dragging Myrtle's flabby body across the bathroom into the tub. He fell onto the bed, reached for the cat and stroked her head. "We're free, Bubbles. We can do anything we want."

He lay there for a minute, feeling his pounding heart begin to quiet. He stared at the empty safe for a long moment. What *did* he want to do for the rest of his life?

He had no friends, no hobbies. The only pleasure in his life was plotting Myrtle's murder and now even that pleasure was gone. He grabbed Bubbles and clutched her to his chest, tears pricking his eyes.

A rush of panic gripped his throat. "What am I going to do now?" A wave of nausea swept through his stomach. "Wait! As soon as she figures out the diamonds are fakes, she'll come back!" The realization hit him like a bucket of ice water.

Everything would be just like before. She'd shriek for incessant cups of coffee. She'd have him fetching and carrying until he'd think his back would break. She'd criticize and berate him. Life would become even more unbearable than before because she'd know he switched the diamonds. *She'll never forgive me!* Terror clutched his heart.

And then he saw the words, as clear as if written on a giant billboard stretching across Sleep Train Arena at a Kings basketball game. *You'll have to kill her!* A warm tingle flowed from his toes to his fingertips. He shivered with anticipation.

She'd be sleeping. He'd take a knife from the kitchen drawer and sneak up the stairs. He'd creep across the room until he stood over her body, and then he'd plunge the knife again and again into her heart. Blood would squirt up and across the duvet and splash onto the nightstand where it would wick into the crocheted doily, then drip over the edge, drip... drip... drip... .

He smiled. He had no choice. This time, he'd have to do it.

ELAINE FABER's short stories are published in several magazines and three anthologies, with two more anthologies to be published in spring 2013. She is a member of Sisters in Crime and Inspire Christian Writers Club. Elaine is an editor on the 2012/2013 Inspire Faith Anthologies. She currently seeks publication for three cozy Cat Mysteries. Elaine lives with her husband and four house cats and feeds three more wild critters that come to the door night and morning. She enjoys visiting her Nevada City cabin and receiving writing encouragement from her husband and inspiration from the cats. Visit her at www.MindCandyMysteries.com.

THE BRIDESMAID WORE A BULLET
M. J. GEORGIA

It was three o'clock in the afternoon and my sister was getting married at six. Last month, I'd taken a day off from work so I could spend my hard-earned cash on a rose-pink taffeta bridesmaid's dress. Too bad it would never see the light of day after the wedding. But Sally was my little sister. We'd only had each other since our parents passed away five years ago. I'd already reconciled myself to the fact that I'd have to make sacrifices as her only sibling. We got along like oil and vinegar, with personalities and hair to match. Sally was the smooth blond while I was the tart redhead. On the other hand, I always said that together we made a hell of a salad dressing.

My future brother-in-law was a dentist. I warned Sal that dentists had high suicide rates and did she really want to be with a guy who fussed around in people's mouths all day? She told me to shut up and keep writing addresses on the wedding invitations. At least, her kids would have perfect teeth. She'd always been self-conscious about her one crooked front tooth. Dr. Kenneth Lorenzo fitted her mouth with metal braces. A year later, he fitted her left ring finger with a band of gold, diamond attached.

I sat in my hotel room decked out in the frou-frou bridesmaid dress while working on my laptop at a little round table by the bed. The bright Sacramento sun tried its best to make me sweat, but I had the air conditioner turned on—nothing worse than dark half-moons under your arms to mess up wedding-picture esthetics.

The limo would pick us up in about an hour so I had enough time to check my e-mails, especially any from my boss. I felt a little guilty leaving him to fend for himself while I was gone. He had a bad habit of taking on the worst clients if I wasn't there to play interference. Jake was a little quirky. He had a thing for old Humphrey Bogart movies, the ones where Bogey played detective. In real life, my boss, Jake Waters, was a private investigator, and I was his assistant. Not secretary, but assistant, a real one. I was training to be a PI. Jake promised to make me a junior partner when I got my license. I'm sure Nancy Drew was shaking in her saddle shoes.

No desperate e-mails from Jake so far. I closed the laptop, stretched and got up to walk back to Sally's room. I'd left her room earlier because the other five bridesmaids had circled their wagons around the bride as she got dressed. I wasn't needed for a while. Besides, the conversation always gravitated to my love life or lack of one. The way they talked, it made me think that at the age of twenty-six I might as well adopt a dozen cats and live the rest of my life vicariously through reality television.

The sudden sound of firecrackers in the hall had me racing towards the door. Who would set those off in a fancy hotel? I peeked out into the hallway in time to see a man in a black tuxedo run out the exit at the far end of the corridor. A woman lay crumpled face down on the flowered carpeting in a pool of blood. From the fluffy rose-pink spill of fabric surrounding her I knew she was one of Sally's bridesmaids. It hadn't been fireworks. Someone had fired a gun, several times, into a bridesmaid.

I ran to the prone woman just as more doors opened, curious faces staring. Sally in her white, bead-encrusted gown started to move towards the body, shock on her face.

"Sally," I yelled. "Get back in the room! I'll handle this." Her face was pale, but years of me ordering her around as the big sister paid off. She turned obediently and quickly shut the door. I put my head next to the woman's face then gently felt her neck. I couldn't hear her breath or feel a pulse. Blood seeped out of four holes in her back, turning her pink dress red. If there were more bullet wounds, I couldn't see them.

I pointed my finger at a middle-aged guest. "You, the guy in the plaid cummerbund, call 9-1-1." He nodded and ran back into his room. You had to be specific if you wanted help. Otherwise people just milled around uselessly, thinking someone else would do something.

Though I didn't think she could hear me, just in case, I whispered to the fallen bridesmaid, "I'll stay with you until help gets here."

I left the bridesmaid to attend to my sister minutes later when the cops and paramedics started to show up. From the window in Sally's room, I saw two police cars and an ambulance race up the street with lights flashing, only to have to slow as they approached the hotel driveway. They were jammed behind a long white Hummer limo. The limo driver kept looking nervously into his rearview mirror like he didn't know if they were going to bust him or write him a ticket for driving while ostentatious.

Sally sobbed out that the dead bridesmaid was Lauren Hendricks, a college friend of hers from UC Davis. They'd roomed together freshman year. Lauren sadly left before graduating when her grandfather died in Maine and she needed to attend to the funeral details. Though Lauren never came back to Davis, she and my sister had kept in touch. When Sally asked Lauren to be a bridesmaid, Lauren had been happy to fly in from Maine to be in the wedding party. She'd arrived yesterday excited and alive. Today she was dead.

The police took my statement, but I couldn't identify the man running from the scene. I'd only glimpsed the back of his head (he had short light brown hair) and what he was wearing. I thought it could've been someone from our wedding party, or the other wedding party staying at the same hotel this weekend. Or even a member of the serving staff since the waiters wore black tuxedos.

Sally continued crying inconsolably in her room surrounded by the remaining bridesmaids. She vacillated between wanting Ken with her and saying he couldn't see her before the wedding because it'd be bad luck. Finally Ken came in and took her hand saying they'd probably used up all their bad luck before the wedding so it was okay. I gave him a brownie point for that because Sally looked so relieved to see him.

I thought about calling my boss to get his opinion on what had happened, but decided it'd be loony to even think about investigating a murder on my own.

Yellow crime scene tape crisscrossed the hallway like a waiting line set-up at Disneyland or the airport. I knew forensics people would be there shortly. The whole place had been shut down by the cops, even our limo waiting outside, and we had less than an hour to get to the church.

"Sal, I know this is a shock," I said, "but do you still want to go through with the wedding?"

"Of course, she does," Ken replied. I gave him a dirty look that said I wasn't talking to him.

"Sal?" I tried again, ready to stomp on Ken's shiny instep and take away his brownie point if he answered for her again.

Sally looked at Ken, then at me, her eyes red and watery. One of her false eyelashes had started to come loose at the outer corner. Noreen, an observant bridesmaid, was there with a little pink tube of glue ready to mortar down the errant lash.

"I don't know, Sissy," Sally said to me. "With all the guests, the expenses... I guess we should go through with it. What do you think?" She glanced around the room at the other bridesmaids. They hadn't really known Lauren, but they all looked upset and unsure. Finally, Noreen nodded and the rest followed suit.

"I'll have to let Matt know," Ken said. Matt was the groomsman who was supposed to walk with Lauren down the aisle. They'd just met last night at the rehearsal dinner.

"Do you know Lauren's next of kin?" I asked Sally.

"I gave the police the information," she said. "I don't know her parents. I only heard Lauren talk about them. They didn't get along very well."

She looked at me. "I just can't call them, Sis. I just can't."

I patted her on the shoulder. "I understand. The police will take care of it."

I wondered how to get us all out of the room, past Lauren's tarp-covered body and the crowd of police surrounding it, without someone freaking out. It made me realize that no matter what your life was like, whether you liked your privacy and time by yourself, death was not a solitary affair. And you wouldn't be able to do a damn thing about it.

The police wanted statements from everyone in the wedding party before they would let us go, so we were an hour and a half late to the church. I called the priest so he could tell the guests there'd been a delay. Finally, all the women piled in the limo, white and pink skirts flying. I got my hem shut in the door and ended up with a brown streak across the bottom of the gown. I shrugged. It wasn't as if I'd wear it again anyway. The men met us at Saint Bartholomew's. They'd rented two black Lincoln town cars, eschewing a limo as they didn't have a hundred yards of taffeta to contend with like we did.

St. Bart's Church was a grand stone structure dominating a corner in downtown Sacramento. We weren't Catholic or much of anything else approaching an organized religion, but the Lorenzos were, so Sally had agreed to convert to Catholicism. Converting from *what* she didn't share with me. I briefly contemplated popping in at the office which was only a few blocks away to tell my boss what had happened, but I decided I'd have to hurt him if he laughed at my dress, so I stayed where I was.

The wedding went off without a hitch, no pun intended. During the ceremony I tried to see the backs of the men's heads, especially ones with light brown hair. None of them looked familiar. The newly married couple kissed and marched down the aisle. We blew bubbles and threw bird seed at them. Sally looked pretty happy, considering. I wished reality didn't have to intrude. Even as I waved at the departing limo, I wondered why someone had killed Lauren.

The rest of the wedding guests got into cars and taxis to follow to the reception. I rode in Noreen's Honda Civic with two other bridesmaids, hoping she could see out of her windows with all the pinkness blocking her view.

Unfortunately, the reception was being held at the hotel where Lauren was shot. It had seemed like a good idea at the time, as guests could drink all they wanted and just toddle off to their rooms afterwards. Sally and Ken wouldn't have to worry about them trying to drive home. Now, the sight of the hotel made me sad.

Inside the ballroom, I took my seat at one end of the head table, quickly drank my glass of champagne and signaled the waiter over to pour another. The waiter had light brown hair. I stared at him as he poured.

"Is there anything else I can do for you?" he asked, noticing my stare. I shook my head and tried to smile. He walked away to pour wine into other empty glasses.

Noreen leaned over and whispered to me, "He's hunky! I could think of some things he could do for *me*." She giggled. I wasn't the only one slamming down the bubbly.

I looked at Sally and saw she was trying hard to keep her smile going. She laughed dutifully at the jokes the best man cracked as he gave his well-rehearsed toast. As maid of honor, I also gave a toast. It was short, sweet and heart-felt. I'd never liked public speaking. Sally's smile for me was genuine, but her eyes had a glassy sheen from unshed tears. I smiled back, wishing I knew who the son-of-a-bitch was who'd ruined the happiest day of my sister's life.

The music started after the toasts. Sally and Ken took their first dance together as Dr. and Mrs. Lorenzo. Those ballroom dance classes really paid off for them. As others started to join them on the dance floor, I got up to find the ladies' restroom while looking for the waiter with the light brown hair.

I saw him walking down the hallway outside the ballroom carrying an empty tray down by his side. I followed. He opened a door that said "Staff Only" and walked inside. I waited a minute then opened the same door, looking around cautiously before committing myself. The door shut automatically with a soft *snick*. I was in a service corridor that ran behind the hotel's line of ballrooms. No carpeting here, just plain concrete floors and florescent lighting, very utilitarian. Ahead of me, I glimpsed a man turning down a side corridor so I kept walking.

The corridor was dark and empty. Maybe I'd been mistaken. Turning around, I smacked right into his chest. He'd come up silently behind me.

"What do you want?" he asked. "Why did you follow me?"

I stepped back. "I, uh, wanted another glass of champagne?" I mumbled, at a complete loss for words.

"I'm not an idiot. Why did you follow me?"

"I thought you looked like someone I knew." I craned my neck around, looking desperately for other service staff.

"I don't know you."

I smiled, "Right. Well, then, I made a mistake. I guess I'll be going back to the party now." I tried to walk away, but he reached out and grabbed my arm.

"You saw me," he said, sudden realization dawning his face.

"Saw you?" I tried to look innocent. "Uh, yeah, I saw you at the reception. Is that what you mean?"

"Shit. You saw me in the hallway, after the girl got shot."

"No. What hallway? What girl? Someone got shot?" I twisted my arm, testing how determined he was to hold me.

"Don't play dumb. I didn't shoot her, if that's what you think."

"Me? I would never think a thing like that! I really need to get back to the reception. I'm sure they've noticed I'm gone."

"I don't think anyone will notice for a while, not with all the champagne flowing in there."

"My sister's the bride, she'll notice, all right."

"Even so," he said, "she doesn't know where you are now, does she?"

I couldn't think of what to say to that, because it was true. No one knew where I was.

He looked around then pulled me into a small storage area. I inhaled sharply and opened my mouth to scream, but he let go of my arm. "Look, I didn't shoot your friend. I just happened to be there when it happened."

I shut my mouth. This was interesting.

"Did you see who did it?" I asked.

"It was a woman. She ran when she saw me."

"I opened my door right after I heard the shots. I didn't see a woman."

"She ran into the elevator. I started to go after her when I saw a room door open. I guess that was you. I knew it'd look bad for me, so I ran."

"Why not tell the cops what you saw?" I asked. "Why run?"

"I have a police record. It was just kid stuff, but I thought it'd make me look guilty. I didn't want to lose my job. I panicked." He ran a hand through his hair, messing it up, making him look like a teenager.

"What'd the woman with the gun look like?"

"Let me think a minute. She had short blond hair, medium height, slim, maybe in her thirties." He ran his hand through his hair again. I noticed he had nice blue eyes.

"What was she wearing?"

"I don't know, maybe pants and a sweater, dark colors. Look, I didn't stop to take a picture, okay?"

"Yeah, okay." I was starting to believe him. The real murderer wouldn't have bothered to make up a story. I was here with him in the dark, armed with nothing but a pair of rose-pink high heels. If he wanted to shut me up, he could've done it by now.

"We should go to the police and give them the woman's description," I said.

He stood so close to me I could smell the soap he'd used that morning. Irish Spring, I thought. We looked at each other for a moment. He cleared his throat and stepped back. The moment passed.

"No. Please." He looked pleadingly at me with blue puppy-dog eyes, maybe a Husky puppy. "There's a chance the woman is still here in the hotel. If she is, we can tell the police."

I thought about what he'd just proposed. "I kind of hope she isn't," I said.

"Why?" he asked, looking puzzled.

"Because you're a witness to a murder and she has a gun."

We walked out of the utility corridor together, agreeing to meet up again after the reception. We also exchanged names. After our little tête-à-tête, I figured we should at least be on a first name basis. His name was Tom. I wanted to change out of my princess dress before trying to do any more investigating. Just my luck, before I could even get back into the ballroom, Tom came up behind me and pulled me into an alcove.

"What's up? I thought we were going to meet later," I said.

"Shhhh," he whispered. "She's here!"

I looked around. "Where?"

"Over there at the registration desk! She's checking out. We have to do something now!"

A blond woman was standing at the desk, a small black rolling suitcase by her feet. She wore a dark colored tunic, tight black leggings and flats. I guessed it must be what all the trendy murderesses were wearing this season.

"How do we stop her?" Tom asked. His face was scrunched up in a worried frown. He looked kinda cute, but I tried to ignore him as my mind worked furiously.

"I have an idea," I said. "Stay here for a minute then come over when you see me talking to her."

"What're you going to do?" he asked. But I didn't have time to answer him. I had to stop her from leaving the hotel.

I grabbed my full skirt with one hand and waved the other hand frantically over my head as I ran full speed towards her.

"Aunt Jessica! Aunt Jessica! You can't leave yet, the reception just started!" She looked curiously at me, then behind her in case I was talking to someone else.

"Aunt Jessica! Thank goodness I caught you!" I ran up to her and threw my arms around her in a bear hug. She struggled to get loose but, being taller and bigger than she, I hung on successfully.

"Get off of me!" she said, "I'm not your aunt!"

"What a kidder, Aunt Jessica!" I looped my arm through hers and tried to lead her toward the reception. I spied Tom walking in our direction.

"Tom!" I called out. "It's Aunt Jessica!" The woman took one look at Tom and started struggling in earnest.

"Let go of me, you lunatic! I said I'm not your aunt." The woman kicked at my legs. It might have worked if I hadn't been wearing my bullet-proof bridesmaid dress. The yards of fabric softened the blows so I could still hang on to her. Tom came up and took her other arm. I spotted one of the detectives who'd been questioning people earlier that afternoon and steered our little gang toward him. The woman recognized him, too. She went wild, thrashing between us.

"What's going on here?" he asked, walking over and looking at us warily.

"These people are trying to kidnap me!" our prisoner shouted. "Help me please, I-I think this man committed a murder!" She twisted out of our grips as we loosened them in surprise.

Tom immediately countered with, "I *saw* this woman shoot the bridesmaid this afternoon! She's trying to blame it on me."

The detective raised both his eyebrows and took out his cell phone. After a brief call, he hustled all of us into a private office behind the reception desk to wait.

"Better grab her luggage," I offered helpfully, "the murder weapon might be in it."

After more cops had joined us, they separated us into three rooms for questioning. They now had two suspects who were pointing fingers at each other and a third possible accomplice (that would be me). The woman—Rose was her name—kept saying that she saw Tom shoot the bridesmaid. Tom, of course, insisted she'd done the shooting. The cops found a gun in Rose's luggage that was the same caliber as the weapon used to kill Lauren. Forensics would determine if it was the exact gun, but unfortunately, that was enough evidence for them to haul all of us downtown to the station.

After a long while, too many cups of bitter cop-shop coffee and endless questions, all the pieces of Lauren's murder fell into place. The woman was Lauren's father's mistress. Lauren had inherited her grandfather's estate those years ago. Apparently, if Lauren died, the money would go to her father. Rose figured if he had the money, he could afford to divorce his rich wife and marry her. This all came out in Rose's confession. She broke surprisingly fast for someone tough enough to plan a murder. I blamed it on the cop-shop coffee, a form of torture not covered by the Geneva Convention.

Tom had just been in the wrong place at the wrong time. He was doing a favor for one of the other workers, delivering a package to a guest on the same floor as our wedding party. We found out we lived only a few blocks from each other and agreed to go for coffee the next weekend. And the weirdest thing was I started liking my bridesmaid dress. I thought I'd make a nice set of pillow covers out of it for my bedroom, as a keepsake from my first murder investigation.

M. J. GEORGIA is a published author and film noir buff. She has a passion for old black-and-white movies from the '40s and '50s, depicting hard-boiled gumshoes and shady dames. Her mysteries often contain humor. Her quirky characters make her laugh quietly to herself as she writes, often to the discomfort of other coffee house patrons. Further adventures of Jake and Sissy of the Waters and Bridges Agency will be available soon. Visit her website at www.Mertianna.com to read her blog and learn about her urban fantasy Synemancer series set in the San Francisco Bay Area, featuring magic, strange happenings and dangerous characters.

A SIMPLE QUESTION
EVE IRELAND

Connie walked straight through the riverfront restaurant's dining room and used both arms to push open double doors to the sunny al fresco deck. Only someone with her petite form could pull off the fitted black leather pants and tailored white linen jacket that hugged her midsection. Her shiny yellow hair bounced on her shoulders as she walked on her toes to keep the skinny heels of her short black boots from lodging in gaps between the planks. She studied the available tables and pulled out a chair beneath a grass-colored umbrella at the far end of the dining space. A young waiter placed a paper napkin on the granite-topped wrought iron table and took her iced tea order. Connie slid a cell phone from her jacket pocket and set it on the glassy surface.

It was early afternoon in Sacramento and only a few of the Capitol lunch crowd remained. Her husband had flown out that morning for a business trip; the kids would be in school a couple more hours.

Before making a game-changing phone call, she sat back and watched the calm river, appreciating the beauty of its glimmering surface but well aware of unseemly activity churning beneath the muddy water. By the time a paddlewheel boat cruised by, her beverage had been delivered. She took a sip, then picked up her smart phone, located the contact on the display screen and pressed the number to call. Connie wasted no time when it was answered.

"Did you and Jack ever have an affair, Mary?"

"What? Who is this? Connie? Oh, my goodness, is that you? How did you get this phone number?"

"You *gave* it to me a couple of years ago. Am I not supposed to call

33

you on your cell phone?"

"No, it's okay. A phone number didn't show up on the screen so I didn't know who it was. I haven't heard from you for so long. I'm so surprised."

"Really?" The word stretched with sarcasm. "So?"

"I'm just parking my car and heading into a business meeting. In... Los Angeles. So how are you? What's up? Are you coming to Santa Barbara?"

"Answer the question, Mary. Did you have sex with my husband? Ever?"

"Whoa, hello to you, too. I thought you were joking! Talk about out-of-the-blue."

"I want the truth. And I want to hear it directly from the whor— horse's mouth."

"I would never do that." The pitch of Mary's voice raised an octave. "Why are you asking? My god. How long have you thought this?"

Connie listened with disinterest. "Pretty much since I've known you," she said dryly. "What's that? About twenty-three years?"

Connie imagined Mary's panic, her dazed green eyes, and her usual pasty complexion draining to a translucent white that would make her long brunette locks appear even darker.

Decades before, when Mary was a regional manager for a large retail chain, she'd hired Connie as a division manager in the Santa Barbara store. Connie soon learned that Mary always had an agenda. In Connie's case, Mary had hired a bright and well-connected socialite, and she'd exploited her new hire by initiating an off-duty friendship. Connie had been hesitant to turn her down since Mary was her boss.

They were young, upwardly mobile couples, early in their careers, early in their marriages. Mary insisted that they take turns hosting dinners at each of their homes on the weekends. In time, other co-workers and friends were invited to Saturday night gatherings and the nucleus expanded. As jobs changed and couples moved away, their weekend dinners were held less often. Still, Mary called frequently to keep their social friendship alive. Even when they lived in different cities, weekend dinners were assembled as major gastronomic events for three or four couples to enjoy once or twice a year. Long before Martha Stewart, Connie was the Queen of Creative and a master of exotic dishes and experimental chocolate desserts. Jack's extensive wine cellar easily added complementary beverages to unveil the scents and flavors of each innovative course.

After their third baby arrived, Connie and Jack embarked on new careers and moved their family to Sacramento. Whenever Connie missed the coast, Mary would invite her south to their beachfront Montecito home for a girls' weekend. Their long conversations would always include the men in their lives. For Connie, that meant sharing her frustration with full-time work and the sometimes-thankless job of caring for a husband and children. Since Mary and her husband, Gene, had no children at the time, Mary talked about the men she was screwing behind her husband's back. Or maybe in front of his face. Whichever, it was information that Mary demanded Connie take to her grave.

Confidential sharing while walking along sand dunes near Mary's showcase home or shopping at downtown boutiques couldn't hide the undercurrent in their friendship. After all, Mary had begun flirting with Jack at their very first dinner party. She couched her questions in an innocent tone, asking how things were with Jack, or what Connie would do if she ever found out Jack had been unfaithful, but Connie could see how anxious Mary was for answers.

During these private "girl talks," Connie toyed with Mary and intentionally made such comments as, "Well, you know, accidents happen," just to see Mary's expression. Connie especially enjoyed the time she answered, "People black out when they're temporarily insane," and watched Mary's face turn from interest to horror.

The evening of Mary and Gene's first visit to Connie and Jack's new Sacramento home, the two couples dined at The Firehouse Restaurant. After food had been ordered and drinks freely poured, Mary left for the powder room. Moments later, Jack excused himself while Connie and Gene continued chitchat until they ran out of conversation. A waitress who had been observing their table and waiting to take their orders drifted toward Connie, leaned over, and said in her ear, "Something's going on under the table between the two people who just left."

Connie tried to pass off the stranger's startling and unwanted opinion. She wasn't oblivious to Jack and Mary's behavior, only adjusted. She was sure Jack, over time, would treat her with the respect she deserved and all would be forgiven.

Mary and Jack returned to the table, laughing, but didn't share what was amusing them when Gene asked. Within minutes, Connie felt someone's shoe brush back and forth against her leg and looked directly at Jack's eyes. "What's going on under there?" she asked through gritted teeth.

Instead of meeting her gaze, he looked straight ahead at Mary. "Oh, I was just stretching my legs. Why? Did I kick someone?" Jack and Mary were the only two who laughed.

Only months before, Connie had wanted to end the marriage, but Jack—who represented international banking interests—was as a master negotiator. He begged his wife not to go. In a moment of power, she gave Jack the terms of a trial period for their marriage. She'd been confident that he had complied. Until that night.

Now, years later, Connie waited for a simple, one-word answer through the dead air.

Mary gasped. "Holy shit!"

"What happened?" Connie asked.

"Oh, I was just startled. A man who's going to the meeting just knocked on my car window and scared the crap out of me. He's going into the building."

"Before you go, is there anything you'd like to tell me?"

"Connie, I don't know what to tell you, what to say. I'm stunned."

"That's impossible. You've never been at a loss for words."

"How could you possibly think that I would want Jack? Come on, Connie, he's not my type."

"Oh, that's funny. Are you going to try to tell me that Terry, Tom and John were your *type*?"

"That's not fair, Connie. All of that happened so long ago. I trusted you not to repeat those things."

"I haven't told anyone about your trysts—at least the ones I know about. But that doesn't make them disappear. All I want to know is what happened between you and my husband."

"Seriously, Connie. Why would I want him?"

"Good question. But then, you've always had a penchant for acquiring things—diamonds, furs, expensive cars, other women's husbands…"

"You know that I would never do anything to hurt you."

"That's not what I asked you. You know, Mary," Connie paused, "this is your last chance."

"What do you mean?"

"I didn't mumble. This is your last chance to fess up. For all the times I listened to your confessions about affairs, all the times you asked me to never tell Gene and take your tales of immorality to my grave—I'm asking you a simple question, and for the truth about your not-so-secret meetings with my husband, and you can't be honest?"

"What do you mean 'meetings'?"

"You thought I wasn't aware of the 'breaks' you'd take from the store when we worked together? Those times when I was pregnant and needed to go home to put my feet up at lunchtime? Those times you said I had to stay and watch the store because you had *plans*?"

"What does that have to do with anything?"

"Are you kidding? Someone is always watching, Mary. *Always*. You remember my neighbor across the street—Gladys? She was more than happy to tell me that she had seen Jack and 'some woman' going into the house during the day. When I asked, she described *your* car."

"So?"

"My neighbor told me the two of you were in my home *alone!* You want to explain that to me?"

"There's nothing to explain."

"Really? You've got this 'innocent' routine down pat. Wow. At a box store a couple of years ago when I was on the coast, those same neighbors recognized me. Their first question was to ask if I was still married. They were shocked that I was.

"Okay, Mary, answer me this: why did you and Jack always go missing when we had the other couples over for dinner? After a few drinks and dinner, we'd all notice that the two of you weren't in the room. One at a time, you two would reappear."

"How should I know? Maybe we went to the bathroom."

"Together? How stupid do you think we all were? And how many times did you think your standard answer about where you'd been would work?"

"Standard answer?"

"'We were talking about something confidential' was the line."

"So what's wrong with that?"

"What *'confidential'* conversation could a man possibly have with another woman who wasn't his wife?"

"Connie, how can you expect me to say anything? You've created this fantasy in your mind. It wouldn't matter what I say."

"Try me. I'm giving you the opportunity to cleanse your soul, rise to the occasion. So far, I haven't heard one honest word or anything close to a plausible explanation out of your mouth."

"I can't believe you've held onto these feelings all these years," Mary said.

"I can't believe you don't know you've been embarrassing yourself all these years," Connie retorted. "Let me give you an example. When I had just delivered Jack's and my first son, who went out to dinner with my parents while I was recovering in the hospital?"

"It was a celebration dinner. I would have expected you to do the same if the situation were reversed," Mary said.

"You thought it was okay to go to *my* celebration dinner? What the hell were *you* celebrating? Do you know what my mother and father's first question to me was when they returned to Cottage Hospital?"

"Of course, not," said Mary.

"They asked me what was going on between you and Jack."

"Why would they say that?"

"Because at dinner, you said to Jack—*in front of my parents*—'Oh, Jack, if Connie wasn't around, you'd go for *me*, right?'"

"I said that? It was probably the wine talking."

"Drunk or not, you said it and they passed it along to me. Imagine the humiliation and the sheer terror I experienced in my hormonal state. Why were you there anyway? You weren't a godmother or anything. It's because you always invited yourself along where you weren't wanted. And you rattled the foundations of a lot of marriages in the process."

"But when you guys moved away you said your marriage was better, that the whole family was better."

"Did you ever ask yourself *why* we moved, Mary? Why we *really* moved?"

"What do you mean?"

"I insisted we move somewhere else for better careers because I wanted our family to get the hell away from *you*."

"Why didn't you ever say something?"

"You were my *boss*, Mary! You know what the laws were like twenty years ago. If I'd made the claim and even had photo proof, a legal decision still would have gone against me. I would have lost my job, not you. I was looking out for my family."

"This is incredible."

"No, *you're* incredible. You're a parasite, Mary, simple white trash."

"So why did you stay friends with me?"

"Are you kidding? I think you're the one who taught me to keep my friends close but my enemies closer. How else would I know where my husband was?"

"This can't be happening."

Connie laughed. "It's been *happening* for a lifetime. All I'm asking is for you to own up to it." She sank deep into her patio chair, relishing the mild northern California sun peeking through puffy clouds, and took a sip of tea. A gentle breeze coaxed soft ripples of mossy river water to lap against wood pilings deep beneath the deck.

The silent moment gave way to Mary's protest. "Wait a minute. How could you possibly think anything was going on between Jack and me? You're the one who let him stay at my house when he came over for business trips."

"I didn't *let* Jack stay there—he passed it off as cost-savings for the company. You know what I'm really wondering?"

"I give up."

"Now that you have a child of your own, a daughter, how are you going to raise her? Are you going to raise her to be a tramp like you?"

"Leave my daughter out of your insults!"

"Mary, you've insulted me as long as I've known you. I'm pretty sure you have the capacity to receive a little of your own medicine. You never said Gene is the father."

"Oh, my god!"

"Maybe she's Jack's."

"Connie! How could you! Hope is Gene's daughter!"

"Only if that's what the paternity test says. Did you ever take one? Hope. I always wondered about that name. Are you *hoping* that she'll turn out differently than you?"

"I think this conversation is over."

"Mary, rest assured, this conversation will be ringing in your ears for eternity. It's time you take responsibility for deliberately ruining many people's lives for your selfish pleasures. Do you even know the definition of 'repent?' How about 'contrition?' After all, you're the one who seems to believe that you can sin day in and day out, then confess to your priest and the sun will break through the clouds and shine on you. Do you think you can just do what you want, take what you want, and that there'll never be consequences? How sick is that?"

"Look, I know I've made mistakes. I've even shared some of my bad decisions with you because I trusted you. But I would never hurt you."

"Oh, but you have. And I'm telling you that you have. But, for some reason, putting the facts on the table, which have been verified by observers I didn't even know, doesn't seem to matter. You're acting as though you're not a part of it. Why, exactly, is that?"

Connie heard a series of booming thuds.

"What's going on there, Mary?"

"That person who was pounding on my car window is at it again, waving me into the meeting. I'm going to have to go."

"Before you do, how are we going to resolve this conversation?" Connie could hear sniffles. She imagined uncontrollable tears running down Mary's pale cheeks and loved it.

"Is there a resolution?" Mary paused. "Why now, Connie? Why in the world are you throwing all of this on me now, today of all days?"

"Because time's up, Mary," Connie said matter-of-fact. "This can't go on another second. It's time to admit it, get it over with and appease at least some of the damage you've done in your life."

Connie could feel Mary considering her response. She didn't want to lose momentum. "Mary?" Connie moved from her shaded table to lean over the deck railing and watched a mallard and her four goslings skimming the muddy river water. "When my children ask me if I love their daddy, I'd like to be able to tell them 'yes' and really mean it. The only way I'm going to be able to put this behind me is to know the absolute truth so I can accept it, face it and move on."

Silence.

"That sounded like sea gulls," Mary said. "Are you close by?"

"They're gulls, but I'm not by the sea." Connie was sarcastic. "We *do* have waterways up here in the yonder northern territories.

"Look. I know there have been many times over the years that you've wanted to say things to me, tell me things about Jack. Come on, Mary, it's time."

Mary was silent again for a moment, then she said, "Do you remember what you told me you'd do if you ever found out that Jack was cheating?"

"I do," Connie said with cheer.

"For god sakes, Connie, you told me 'accidents happen.' Now, how am I supposed to deal with that? I'm not saying I ever did anything wrong, but what if I was aware of something and told you? How could I know that you wouldn't do something violent? Something unspeakable?"

Like a mother to a child, Connie said, "Mary, there are no guarantees in life. Am I right?"

"So?"

"So, there's no way to know how anyone will respond to a crappy hand they're dealt. You're a woman of faith. You're just going to have to trust."

"Do you remember telling me that you could shoot Jack and his lover and not go to jail by calling it a momentary fit of insanity?"

"Yeah."

"Well, that scares me about you."

Connie burst out. "That's funny!"

"What on Earth about *that* could possibly be funny?"

"Mary. If two people are willing to violate all of the religious Golden Rules, all rules of friendship, trust and morality, regardless of the consequences, well, those people must be fearless. So, it's funny that you could be *scared* of anything. Aren't you simply saying you're scared of yourself?"

Silence.

"Mary, how good would it feel to have the weight of buried secrets off of your mind? To have some of your past transgressions forgiven? Do you see where I'm coming from?"

"Yeah, I guess—Jesus!"

"What?"

"That business guy is pounding again—he wants to get into the car. Hold on." Connie could hear Mary's muffled voice saying "Just wait—

I'm on the phone with my friend… Connie. I'll come in there in a minute."

Connie's phone vibrated in her hand. On the display was a GPS tracking text for one of the family cell phones.

"So, who is that really, Mary?"

"What do you mean?"

"He can see you're on the phone. Why is a business associate so persistent?"

"Look, Connie, I'm really sad that you've held on to all of these bad feelings. I wish you would have shared this with me sooner, but when you've been holding onto suspicions like this for so long, I don't think there's anything I can tell you to make you feel better. Are you sure you're not just feeling a little down?"

"Wow. Do you know what Jack's favorite song is? It's "Deny, Deny, Deny." I've always hated country music—the old 'my wife left me, dog died, lost my job, and drinkin' my sorrows away' crap. But Jack's always loved it. He's always been a fan of telling me that I've got a wild imagination.

"Can I tell you something, Mary? When other people have to point out that you're not seeing the slime you're walking in, you become the fool. The plain, simple truth is that I'm not willing to be the fool anymore. I'm done. The real Connie is back—the one before I married a liar and a cheat. The one before a whore who sleeps with all of her friends' husbands befriended me. Do you think that none of the wives know what you've done? Do you think Gene has never been suspicious? Well, I'm done. It's that simple."

"Wait, just a second. That business guy wants to get into the car while we finish our conversation. There's a bad storm moving in. It's really cold and windy outside."

Connie heard the clunk of an automatic car door mechanism.

"Okay, were we just about done?"

"Mary, it's 70 degrees and sunny in Los Angeles. But it's cloudy with thunderstorms predicted on the central coast. And GPS tracking is as common as chewing gum."

"I'm not following."

"Did you have, are you *continuing* to have, an affair with my husband?"

"I just don't have an answer."

Connie hit the forward key to send a prepared text message, "still deny," to a distant pre-charged cell phone. Some women bonded in love, caring and friendship; others bonded in hatred. And a team of scorned women was more furious—and deadly—than a raging wildfire.

"Too bad. I do. Goodbye, Mary."

Connie pitched her pre-charged cell phone into the Sacramento River and walked into the restaurant's bar. She had just enough time for her favorite vodka martini, straight up with two olives, before heading home to start dinner for the kids. She knew that Gene would be picking up his daughter from school near Montecito at about the same time. Connie tipped the martini glass and contemplated a celebratory getaway with her *real* girlfriends.

Mary's parking space, tucked beneath a one hundred-year-old oak, was shielded by a mature hedge wall and provided the seclusion the paramours were seeking in the back lot of the Biltmore. Also shielded was the petite figure in a black camouflage jumpsuit and hood who, from an adjacent branch, had full windshield view to assure the lovers would never enjoy their regular meeting.

A deep explosion of thunder inside the black skies unleashed a lightning-filled cloudburst along the Santa Barbara shoreline, echoing the crackling screeches of the angry sirens. Waves of hail slamming the asphalt parking lot muffled the rupture of fatal gunshots just as the first bullet hit the crown of Mary's parietal skull and stunned her. Her consciousness faded within moments of the second bullet entering her right frontal lobe and exiting the temporal bone near her left ear. The county coroner determined that the man died of the first gunshot behind his right eye, though he found a second slug in the man's neck. He was unable to explain the redness on Jack's knuckles.

The slumped bodies went unnoticed for hours as hotel guests in the distance scattered like ants trying to find shelter from the deluge.

EVE IRELAND is the pen name of a career communications professional and freelance writer/editor. She has been an award-winning member of the news media and various publications as well as a public relations leader in several public and private sector industries. Her passion for writing began in elementary school when she won a patriotic essay. Mysteries are her favorite genre, and she currently is working on a political thriller set in Sacramento. She can be reached at Eve.Ireland@gmail.com.

CORPSE POSE

R. FRANKLIN JAMES

"Breathe deeply. Let the air fill your lungs from the bottom of your rib cage and then exhale from the back of your throat." Barbara's soothing voice was putting Grace to sleep. It didn't take much; she was exhausted from back to back, twenty-four-seven weeks. She took a deep breath and slowly let it out.

"Okay, one last time. Good. Now turn over onto your right side, raise yourself with your left hand, and come to an easy sit."

There was a silent shuffle as the six women and one male came into position. Grace opened one eye and took a glance around the dimly lit room. Her hand automatically sought the gun in her purse resting on the floor near her. Then tilting her head, she heard the light breath of snoring. Terry, their newest member, had fallen asleep again.

Barbara had noticed, too. She smiled benignly and said in a sing song, "Terry, Terry, time to wake up."

Terry opened her eyes, jerked up and smiled sheepishly. "Sorry, your voice does it to me every time."

"You're new to yoga," Barbara said. "You'll find it happens to a lot of us here."

Everyone laughed in understanding. They stood and rolled up their mats and straps.

Barbara got out her notebook. "Remember, I'll be going back to my studio tomorrow, and Mark Coulter is returning to lead your class." She looked around the room. "I've really enjoyed being a substitute, and you have been a great class. I learned a lot from you as well."

Grace made a mental note to wear her new yoga pants tomorrow.

"Oh, yeah," Barbara added, "whoever left the votive candle set—thank you. I really like it."

Grace raised her eyes to the ceiling. It had to have been Myra. She was always kissing up. You'd think they were in high school, not forty-somethings trying to hold on to some semblance of youthful vigor.

Myra smiled shyly, "I just thought it would add to the restful atmosphere here."

Give me a break.

Leaving the studio, they all said goodnight at the foot of the pathway and headed to their cars in the lot. The evening air had a chill and the fleeting smell of honeysuckle rose gently from the vines woven throughout the cyclone fence. Grace saw one of the neighbors staring. She stared boldly back. The elderly woman sniffed and returned to raking the leaves that dotted her yellowed grass.

Namaste to you, too.

"Grace, wait." Terry came up to her, pulling her hoodie over her sleeveless yoga top.

Grace leaned against her car. "Hey, what's up?"

Terry lowered her voice. "Do you still work for Sigma Overton?"

Sigma Overton, known to its workers as Sigma, was a little-known private company that paralleled a similar division under Homeland Security. Highly top secret and definitely off the news grid, even the company's name was confidential. It rankled and worried Grace that Terry knew about it, and her. She had told no one about her work.

"Yes, why?"

"I know about Prospectus."

Grace could feel the smile freeze on her face.

"How?"

Prospectus was a computer simulation protocol that modeled intrusions or, in simpler terms, traced or monitored high risk hackers. Using a combination of satellite technology and manufactured radio waves, any computer, cell phone, tablet, or GPS system could be accessed from any country around the globe.

"How do you think?" Terry replied.

Grace's heart beat a rapid staccato in her ears almost drowning out the night sounds. She squinted at the street lights as they gradually came on.

Grace retorted, "I don't know, that's why I asked." A deep breath cleared her thinking. "What do you want?"

"A job."

This was blackmail. "I don't think this qualifies under the President's economic stimulus package," Grace said. "You could go to jail under the national security section."

Terry came toward her. She stopped less than an arm's distance away.

"A meeting—a meeting with Sheffield, that's all I want."

For now. Grace couldn't stop the thought.

The next morning, she faced the head of Sigma with some trepidation.

"She said my name?" James Sheffield did not pause from briskly tapping the key board in front of his monitor even as his dark piercing eyes held Grace's own.

"Rolled off her tongue like honey."

"What's your sense of her?"

Grace bit her bottom lip. "She's cool as ice. She can portray herself as your everyday soccer mom, or she could have what it takes to be an assassin."

He straightened. "Is she?"

"An assassin?"

He glanced up at the ceiling. "No, a soccer mom, what do you think? Of course, an assassin. Do we know anything about her? Have you run her?"

She took a deep breath. "I tried, but evidently I don't have her real name."

Sheffield stared past her. He slammed a folder on his desk. "We've got to get on top of this. Prospectus is due to roll out on Monday. Our clients will not be happy if there's been a leak. Make a meet for tomorrow at 4:30 at the Hyatt near the Capitol. It should be fairly busy with workers stopping for a drink before going home." He scribbled a note and handed it to Grace. "Get Daniel on this. The three of us will meet today in my office after lunch."

It was not that she didn't like Daniel. He was actually very personable. But they were in a competition for alpha dog II, and right now they were tied neck and neck. Later that day, Daniel pushed a bag of chips over to her side of the desk as they sat in his office. Grace was always surprised that Sigma's brightest mind was a social nerd.

Grace shook her head. "Chips are a little too greasy for me."

"Not a problem, more for me." He reached back over for the bag. "Okay, let's see what we can find out about her in time for our meeting with Sheffield. Did she touch your car at all?"

"No, no prints. She stood away." Grace flipped to a page in her note pad. "I called my yoga teacher last night to ask for her e-mail address. Class members get e-mail blasts from him from time to time."

"And?"

"I'm having Kevin run a tracer on it. But I don't hold out much hope. If she can break into Prospectus, she can easily disguise her online ID."

Daniel flinched. "Don't say she broke into Prospectus. It's like nails running down a blackboard."

"What about running a security scrub on her cell phone? We might be able to triangulate where she's located." Grace wrote herself another note. "It's a long shot because I won't be able to track it until we get our hands on her contact number. It's also unlikely it's for real."

"Do what you've got to do. We all have to. The chief has kept me focused on the Prospectus launch. We're in the critical last few days and we've come too far to have anything put the project at risk." He crumpled up the chip bag and tossed it toward the trash can, where it fell to the floor. "Don't worry about me. I know my job. Yours is to get her to the hotel."

"I'll see her tonight at yoga and confirm."

Mark Coulter's voice was as sonorous as Barbara's. "Get whatever props you need, and let's prepare for *Ardha Chandrasana* or Balancing Half-Moon pose."

Grace purposefully sat next to Terry and gave her a wide smile.

Terry wiped her forehead with a small towel "Well, am I a go?"

Grace frowned. "Not here, I'll talk to you outside."

Terry smiled knowingly, gathered her hair in a band and lay down for meditation. Grace noticed Terry's quiet breathing, then the gentle snore. Grace found herself lulled by the drift of Mark's voice and fell into her own deep breathing pattern.

After class, Grace leaned against Terry's car, wishing she had a piece of tape she could lay across her door handle. There was a good chance she could get a decent set of prints.

"What's your full name?" she asked Terry.

"Suzanne Russo, and that's all I'm going to tell you until I see Sheffield."

Grace juggled her yoga mat and strap, then let her water bottle and mat fall to the ground while she dug inside her purse for her car keys. When she picked up the mat, the keys fell. Terry picked up the water bottle and handed it over.

Grace smiled a thank you, then asked, "Is that your real name?"

"No, not really, but it will get you a little closer to the truth."

Grace sighed. "Fine."

"Look, don't get frustrated. I'm not a novice at this, and I don't have a lot of time. In fact, you can tell your boss that there is very little time left for him to hear what I've got to say. It's for his own good and for the whole Prospectus team."

"Ah, so we've moved on to threats?"

Terry or whatever her name was frowned and gave Grace a knowing look.

"No, of course, not, no threat, just it is what it is." She got into her car. "Tell Sheffield I'll tell him everything he wants to know when I see him."

Grace told her about the four-thirty meet at the Sacramento Hyatt.

Terry nodded, then shrugged. "Oh, I get why he chose that place."

Grace stepped back as Terry-Suzanne or whatever maneuvered her car out of the parking lot and was gone.

She checked the time on her cell phone and punched in a number.

"Okay, she's agreed. Start surveillance in Capitol Mall Park across from the hotel and the café on the corner. I'm coming in with prints and a license number. I'm taking them straight to Daniel. Let Sheffield know."

An hour later, Grace walked into Daniel's office again.

"There's nada." Daniel rolled his chair back from the computer screen to face Grace. "I've searched her prints on every covert database on the planet."

"What about the car?"

He gave her a grimace. "It's a rental. She used the phony name she gave you."

Grace shook her head. "How can that be? She bragged she wasn't a novice. She has to have some kind of record."

"Maybe she's pro enough to keep a low profile." Daniel put his hands behind his head. "We don't have a choice. We're going to have to wait to see what she wants."

"You tell that to Sheffield. He's not going to allow access to him without knowing what could be at stake. "

"She said she'd tell him everything at the meeting tomorrow. It doesn't give us any time to vet her, let alone discover her motivations."

Grace nodded. "All right, let's go explain the situation to Sheffield."

He wasn't happy.

Daniel sat stiffly in the leather chair across from Sheffield's desk. "Do you want us to back you up? I don't think it's a good idea for you to meet with her alone."

Grace looked up. "Wait, she didn't say anything about meeting you alone. I think I should go with you."

Sheffield got up from his chair and walked over to the window. The evening's sunset cast an orange and red glow over his face and into the office. He turned back to his anxious staff.

"I'll talk to the chief and let him know we may have a leak. Daniel, you arrange for a tracking team to follow us, then her after the meet. Grace, you'll accompany me. It will make her feel relaxed." He returned to tapping on his keyboard then looked up. "Oh, and Grace, bring your firearm."

Grace found herself nodding again.

"Jim, she said she wanted a job. She might be able to show us where Prospectus has a break. Not that I think there is one," she added hastily.

Jim Sheffield had a reputation for a flash temper.

"Do you honestly think I would give a stranger access to Prospectus to show us a break that they probably made up or put there anyway?" He pulled out a remote and clicked a button. A large screen scrolled down from the ceiling. What appeared to be a graphic of a multi-columned bar chart flashed, waxed and waned as if alive. "After Monday, we'll be able to gain full access over global communications."

Grace noticed his mounting intensity. "Aren't you worried that you're the only one who knows all the call-up protocols? If anything happened to you, it—"

"We've been through this," he said with irritation. "It's only until we get through the test on Monday, then I've arranged for a secure electronic vault."

Sheffield used his laser pointer to pass over the numbers. "Our guys have been pulling all-nighters for weeks cloaking Prospectus' entry points. I know you two have been working double overtime, too, to get things ready. We cannot fail. We cannot let some--some last minute worries throw us off track."

Grace stood. "Don't worry. We know what's needed."

She and Daniel moved toward the door.

"Wait," Jim Sheffield said. "Thanks."

They each gave him a little smile.

The Sacramento Hyatt Hotel, located across the street from the state Capitol, had a large lobby with a casual and comfortable sitting area with a registration desk on one side and a dimly lit bar on the other. In the bar, a crowd of men and women in suits shared tales of their legislative accomplishments for the day. Laughter was plentiful and ice tinkled in glasses.

Grace and Sheffield chose two small couches backed against a wall, facing the sliding glass entrance doors. She marveled at Jim's cool demeanor. He might get rattled over a staff briefing, but at crunch time, he was ice. She found herself going over in her mind what evidence Terry might have. Prospectus was tightly guarded and yet it was no longer exclusively theirs.

Exactly at four-thirty, the double doors opened. A young woman came toward them.

Grace frowned. "That's not her." She spoke into the hidden lapel mic on her shoulder. She sensed Jim stiffen as he mumbled what sounded like a profanity.

The woman smiled. "Hello," she said, "are you James Sheffield?"

She was a tall statuesque blonde with her hair in Rasta braids. She wore jeans and a white tee shirt with a black cotton jacket.

Jim stood and pointed to the chair next to him. "First, who are you?"

"Kathy Moss." She sat on the arm of the seat. "I told Terry I'd come by and tell you that she needs to reschedule your meeting to later today. Something came up and, no, I don't know what it was. I'm just doing this favor."

Grace did everything she could to keep her mounting impatience from her voice. "Why you? How do you know Terry?"

Kathy took a deep breath. "Look, I just work upstairs at the coffee station. We're friends, that's all."

"What time and where?" Sheffield's tone made it clear he had had enough.

Kathy picked up on it, too. "The grove in Miller Park next to the park n' ride lot at eight." She looked down at her cell phone. "I've got to get to work."

After she left, Grace and Jim looked at each other.

"Have her followed," he said. "I don't think she knows anything, but we don't have the luxury to suppose."

Grace nodded and spoke again into her lapel. They walked out and paused on the sidewalk.

"She's a smart lady." He slipped on a pair of dark sunglasses. "The park is public and private at the same time. Post a couple of our team out of sight." He looked down at his phone. "I've got an appointment at six. I'll be twenty minutes away from the meet site. Set things up the way they need to be. I'll meet you at the lot at seven fifty-five."

"Jim, I wonder if we have it wrong—"

He cut her off. "See you this evening."

One of the things Grace liked best about Sacramento was the sunsets. She sat in her car in the lot at Miller Park and felt herself drawn to the waning light. It was a moment before she noticed movement out of the corner of her rear view window: Terry or Suzanne or whoever.

She watched as Terry, along with a young man and a woman, smoothed down the lawn area adjacent to the lot and quickly rolled out what appeared to be some type of sod material that closely resembled the grass it lay on.

They looked around. Grace slid down in her seat.

Terry lifted a small metal box out of a duffel bag and carefully placed it beneath a nearby shrub. Grace took the opportunity to call her location into the office and describe what she was seeing. She jumped when she heard two quick taps on her window. She pushed the open lock on the passenger door.

Sheffield slid into the seat. "Glad to see you got here early. What's going on?"

"I don't know," Grace murmured, squinting into the darkness. "They're setting up something. I can't figure it out yet."

"We're nine minutes from meet time," Sheffield said as he bent down to check the gun in his ankle holster.

Grace watched Terry and her two colleagues huddle together then move apart. Person One of Interest and Person Two of Interest moved back into the bushes. Only Terry remained. She was wearing a charcoal gray running suit and bamboo flip flops. But what caught Grace's attention was the small matchbook-size box she clamped on to her wrist.

Sheffield opened the door. "Enough. We're done with this. Let's go."

They walked quickly across the lawn.

Terry came up to them with an outstretched hand. "James Sheffield? I'm Suzanne Russo, but you can call me Terry."

He didn't take her hand. "Whoever you are, I don't have a lot of time. What do you want?"

Terry was unfazed. "Didn't Grace tell you?"

Grace stayed back, keeping her eye on the bushes. "I couldn't have told him, Terry, I don't know myself."

Sheffield's hand ran over his hair. "What do you know about Prospectus?"

"I know that Prospectus is a highly secret project that could upset the balance of world power." She took a step forward but stepped back when he did.

"What do you want?" Sheffield growled.

Out of habit, Grace turned to look over her shoulder to make sure there were no unwelcome visitors.

Terry licked her lips. "I want a job."

Grace incredulous, sneered, "What kind of job?"

Terry smiled. "Okay, guys come out."

Both Grace and Sheffield quickly drew their nine mm Sig Sauers as the bushes parted and Person 1 and Person 2 tumbled out in rolling somersaults. They moved quickly through what Grace recognized as a *Vinyassa* pose: Sun Salutation.

They stopped abruptly at the sight of the guns.

Terry started speaking rapidly. "Wait. We don't mean any harm. In fact, I wanted to give you an example of what I can do."

She bent over the shrub and pushed what sounded like a button on a tape machine, from which new age music wafted soothingly.

Sheffield chambered a round in his pistol.

For the next few minutes, Grace and Sheffield stood aghast as Terry and company went through a series of yoga postures.

"What the hell," Sheffield murmured.

They holstered their guns.

"Let me talk to her." Grace put out her hand in a "stop" gesture. "Terry, Mr. Sheffield is very busy. He doesn't make a practice of coming into the field. What's going on?"

"Okay, okay. I know who he is. I got this idea that you guys work in a high stress, highly dangerous job. Day after day, your stress levels build without relief." She pointed at them. "Look, you're all ready to kill us, always on high alert. Your judgment can become impaired; soon your problem-solving skills are degenerated."

Sheffield looked up to the sky. "Could you make your point?"

"Mr. Sheffield, look around you. We are living in the most beautiful state in the country. We are experiencing the most beautiful sunset. But you and your team miss it." Terry's voice rose with enthusiasm. "Yoga is an inexpensive, effective, targeted program to relieve stress. One or two sessions a week can increase your team's productivity tenfold."

Sheffield looked over at Grace then turned back to Terry. "How did you hear about Prospectus? Right now that's causing me a lot of stress and I don't see yoga as the answer."

Terry looked sheepish. "I don't want to get her into trouble, but Grace talks in her sleep. I heard her during our yoga class."

Grace's eyes grew wide and she heard her blood roar in her ears.

Sheffield looked over at her in disgust. He raised his wrist and spoke into a silver and black band, "Squad A & B, return to headquarters. The situation is neutralized."

"Jim, I didn't—" Grace faltered.

"Grace, I think we've spent enough time here."

Sheffield turned back to Terry and the two yoga practitioners. "Miss whatever your name is, this is not the way to secure a contract with our organization. We are not interested in working with you. In fact, I want my people always on edge, not engaged in an activity that would dull their reflexes."

"I was afraid you would say that." Terry reached down into her sport bag, pulled out a specially-designed gun and shot him in the center of his forehead. A second later, she followed with another shot between Grace's disbelieving eyes.

"We thought your vanity and curiosity would draw you out into the open," Terry said to the two people on the ground.

They weren't dead, only in a dead sleep.

In a matter of minutes, she and her crew collected the Sigma guns, replaced their victims' suits and shoes with workout clothes and arranged the bodies on the yoga mats. There was an accommodation for the section that eliminated Sheffield's Sigma Overton, and this prize now belonged to them.

At first, the Department hadn't believed Mark Coulter's claim that there was something odd about a new member of his yoga group, but when they planted their operative, Barbara, she reported back to headquarters that known Sigma agent, Grace, indeed murmured in her sleep in class. Terry fought for the yoga sting, and it had worked.

Terry's real name was Jenna. She stepped back, looked around the scene and smiled to herself. Her section was even more secret than Sigma. Known to only a few as operating under Homeland Security, her unit located and isolated the worst international cyber criminals and left them for local authorities to "capture."

It wouldn't take the FBI or local police long to realize what they had stumbled on. Especially when helped by her 9-1-1 messages timed for delivery in fifteen minutes.

Terry smiled down at the figures dressed in yoga outfits. They looked so peaceful in *Shavasana*: Corpse Pose.

R. FRANKLIN JAMES grew up in the San Francisco East Bay Area and graduated from the University of California, Berkeley. Her debut novel, *The Fallen Angels Book Club*, was published recently by Camel Press. She and her husband live in Northern California with their English Springer Spaniel, Bailey. Find R. Franklin James on the web at www.RFranklinJames.com

AMONG STRANGERS
TERESA LEIGH JUDD

Elaine walked along the sidewalk smiling at each person who passed. She wasn't particularly happy. It was a Monday and she was headed to work, another day of waiting on tourists, answering questions about Old Sacramento and enduring one hundred degree heat. The smile was in case someone she knew approached. She'd found it served as a greeting for most people, and they would greet her in return, not knowing she had no idea who they were unless she recognized the voice. She struggled every day to seem friendly without letting people know that she couldn't recognize them by sight. She had suffered her entire life with her strange disorder and only recently learned that there were other people out there who also had "face blindness," an inability to recognize peoples' features.

The old boardwalk clacked beneath her feet as she approached a small gift store. She took a deep breath as she entered. Once there, she no longer had to fear uncomfortable encounters, and it was with a sense of relief that she took her place behind the counter. Here almost everyone she spoke to was a tourist. She wasn't expected to recognize them. The few people who did revisit were not necessarily people she knew.

The shop specialized in souvenirs and was primarily run by her. The owner, Anna, a small Asian woman, distinctive in her accent and attire, accepted Elaine's problem.

Later Monday, a man entered. He was tall and well-dressed in khakis and a green golf shirt.

"Elaine!" he exclaimed. "Good grief. Who would have guessed I would run into you here?"

Pretending to know who he was, she answered, "I've been working here for awhile. I like the constant flow of people from all parts of the world."

Then she waited for him to fill her in on their relationship.

But he didn't.

"It's been such a long time," he said, "I almost didn't recognize you."

"Yes. Well, I have the same problem sometimes."

"What time do you get off? I'd love to take you for a drink and catch up."

"Around six," she answered. "Um, yes, that would be fun."

What the heck, she thought to herself. He obviously knew her, and it would be fun to go out after work for a change.

"OK. I'll be back then. Is there somewhere you'd like to go?"

"Let's go to the Old City Tavern. It's close. A little noisy, but it's an institution in Old Sac."

"Sounds good. See you then."

With that, he turned and left the store. If only she knew who he was. Someone from college? Or even further back? She would just have to play it by ear and hope things went well. She didn't get asked out often, not that she wasn't attractive, but her inability to recognize people made her seem standoffish. She was in her late twenties and could count on one hand the number of dates she had had. This probably wouldn't go any better than her last date. A disaster, she remembered. On returning from the ladies' room, she went to the wrong table and sat down, unaware that her date was at the next table, and the man she was sitting with was alone only because his date had also gone to the ladies' room. She was too embarrassed to explain and left abruptly when the other woman returned. She never heard from her date again.

At six, the door opened, and the same man entered. Not that she could tell by looking at his face. She had taken special notice of what he was wearing and the clothes were the clue she needed to identify him.

"Hi," he said. "Ready to go?"

"Yes. Just let me get my purse." She rescued her bag from the back room. "See you tomorrow, Anna."

"Right. Have a good time." Her boss didn't look up from the pile of receipts she was working on.

The man took Elaine's elbow and steered her past a flock of tourists, around the corner to the bar. Laughter and the din of voices all talking at once greeted them as they entered. Tourists and the after-work crowd filled the long narrow space, and they were lucky to find two seats at the bar.

"I see you know the way," she said as they settled in.

"Checked it out earlier. What would you like to drink?"

"A glass of red wine would be nice."

"Bartender. A glass of your best Merlot and a Jack Daniels on the rocks," he said as the bartender approached.

"So, what have you been doing since I saw you last?" Elaine ventured. It seemed a safe enough question.

"Well, as you know, I was planning on setting the business world afire. Haven't quite made it yet, but I'm doing all right."

"Doing what exactly?"

"Mostly sales. Boring stuff."

So far, no clue as to how she knew him. She tried again.

"And you're living here in Sacramento?"

"No. Still up in the hills."

No help there. She drained her glass thinking to leave before the conversation got embarrassing. "I should be getting home."

"Someone waiting for you?"

"No, but tomorrow is another work day."

"It's early yet," he said to her and called the bartender over. "Could you bring us another couple drinks?"

"Sure thing."

While the bartender was fixing their drinks, Elaine excused herself to go to the ladies room. When she returned, her glass of wine was sitting on the bar in front of her seat. It seemed a little too full so she picked it up carefully and took several sips to avoid spilling any of it. There was a lull in the conversation as they both searched for something to talk about, and to cover the awkward moment, she picked the drink up again and almost drained the glass. She began to feel a little dizzy.

"I think I'd better go now. I'm not feeling too well."

"Oh, that's too bad. Can I give you a lift home?"

"No, I take the train. Thanks, anyway."

"I'll walk you to the station," he said. And that was the last thing she remembered.

She woke in a strange room with a man lying in the bed next to her.

At first, she thought he was sleeping, but then she saw the knife protruding from his chest, the blood on his shirt and his eyes staring open and blank. She slipped out of the bed and discovered that she was partially undressed. All she could think of was getting out of the room as fast as possible. What if the murderer was still there? She saw that it was a cheap motel room and the bathroom door was open. She peeked in and found the room empty. She pulled on her clothes, slid her shoes on and grabbed her purse. She started to leave but then hesitated. Who was this guy, after all?

She found the clothes he had discarded. They weren't the clothes the man she had had a drink with had worn the evening before. Could this be a different man? She found his wallet and pulled out his ID. Duane Parker. Never heard of him. Her date had said he lived in the foothills. This man lived in Redding. Still, the guy she went out with could have lied. He had probably dosed her drink with Rohypnol so lying wasn't out of the question. But the different clothes?

It dawned on her that she might have been set up. She carefully wiped the ID and put it back in his pocket. She didn't know if her fingerprints were on the knife, but she forced herself to wipe the handle. Hands shaking, she used her skirt as a glove, opened the motel door and crept out. She would have been the obvious suspect. Found drugged next to a man she didn't know who may have taken advantage of her. The police were probably on their way already. They would never believe she didn't know the man and couldn't tell if he was the one who had bought her a drink, or another stranger she had picked up later.

Right on cue, she heard sirens in the distance. She ran.

Once on the street, she recognized the area and quickly made her way to a rapid transit station and then home.

The next morning, she scanned *The Sacramento Bee* for news of the murder. Sure enough, there it was, a small story on the inside page. A salesman from Redding had been found stabbed to death in a local motel. Fingerprints had been wiped from the knife and door handles. Otherwise, there were hundreds of prints with no way to tell the recent from the oldest. Elaine exhaled. She hadn't been aware that she was holding her breath. It appeared unlikely that anyone had seen her. But if she hadn't awakened in time, she hated to think what would have happened.

Reviewing the whole episode, it seemed likely that the man who had picked her up had known of her affliction. But how could that be? She'd told very few people. Her family knew, of course, as well as a few close girlfriends, and her boss, Anna. There was her boyfriend in her freshman year of college, a business major, she recalled. She hadn't been able to hide it from him, and at first he thought it was fascinating, but the fascination soon wore off when she often walked right by him, not recognizing him until he spoke. They broke up after about six months. Could this man be her old boyfriend? She couldn't remember his name. Ed? Ed Something. Tears formed in her eyes. Why did this have to happen to her?

At work, she asked Anna if she had seen the man who had come into the shop, but Anna said she had been in the back room the whole time.

She had only heard the conversation.

"Why? Is there a problem?"

"No, no. You know how I am. I just wondered if he was good looking."

"If you can't tell, I guess it doesn't matter," Anna laughed.

"Guess, you're right."

No more was said. The newspaper ran one follow up article stating that the police were questioning a person of interest and would appreciate anyone with information contacting them. Elaine tried to push the whole episode out of her mind and managed to get through some days without giving it a thought. Nights were the worst. Dreams of blood-soaked sheets often awakened her.

Walking to work a couple weeks later, she heard a familiar voice.

"Hello, Elaine."

She gasped. It was the same man. She knew she would never forget his voice. She stepped up her pace, not answering him.

"Got a lucky break, didn't you?" he said. "I didn't think you would come to so soon. Should have called the police right away, but I wanted to make sure I was nowhere near the motel when I did."

Elaine stopped short.

"You killed that man? Why?"

"He was in my way. Always trying to beat my sales record, horning in on my business and, to make matters worse, threatening to tell the company that I was taking a few under the table payments from customers to cut them better deals. He wanted me to turn over the larger accounts to him in exchange for not telling. I couldn't have that."

"But why involve me?"

"I knew you couldn't recognize me or him. One day when Duane and I were working together, we called on the gift store. I recognized you from when we dated in college and immediately realized you were perfect for my plan. Duane had called on the shop more than once so a connection between you could be established. It should have been fool-proof, but you ruined it. Now the police are looking at anyone with a motive so suspicion has fallen on me."

"Why are you telling me this? I can call the police. Tell them who you are and what you said."

"What will you tell them? A man you can't recognize picked you up, drugged you, and you ended up in a motel room with a man you couldn't be sure was the same one you had a drink with. A dead man, at that. Even if they believed your crazy story, you'd still be a suspect. No, I don't think you'll be telling anyone, but in case you decide to tell, just remember, you can't identify me. That was obvious the other night even though you tried to hide the fact. And at any time I can come up and stick a knife in you just like I did to that stupid Duane. You wouldn't have any warning, no chance of running since you wouldn't recognize me coming toward you. Keep that in mind."

With that, he turned and walked away, mingling with several men who had come out of a restaurant. He was right. She could only pick him out by the clothes he was wearing.

It was a nightmare. There must be something she could do, but for the life of her, and she meant that literally, she didn't know what.

The next day a man dressed in sports coat and slacks, accompanied by a uniformed policeman, came into the shop.

"Miss Elaine Sturgis?"

"Yes," Elaine said, her heart sinking into her boots. They had found her.

"I'm Detective Warren. This is Officer Madison. A suspect in a murder case has named you as an alibi. He says he was with you on the night in question."

"When was this?"

"About two weeks ago. Do you recall going to Old City Tavern with this man?" The detective handed her a picture.

Elaine scanned the photo carefully and handed it back to him

"I'm sorry, Detective. I don't recognize him at all."

TERESA LEIGH JUDD is an active member of the Sacramento chapter of Sisters in Crime. She lives in the foothills with her partner, Ken, and has only recently started writing. Short stories are her preferred genre. She has had a number of stories published and is working on a collection, *Dragon Tales*, with a loosely defined dragon theme. More information regarding her published stories and future projects can be found at www.TeresaLeighJudd.com.

MURDER, SELF-TAUGHT
VIRGINIA KIDD

Killing people is just not as easy as it sounds, Jana Matheis thought. Books, for instance, which ought to help you—she scowled at *The Consumer's Guide to Poison Protection*—seemed obsessed with antidotes and emetics and quick, life-saving actions.

She reread her rejection from *Corpses Incorporated.* At least it was a personal letter, not just a preprinted form. She had highlighted "the poisoning of the city council member lacks verisimilitude."

Well, of course it did! How was a nice, middle class, college-educated state employee supposed to know how much cyanide to put in a glass of Beaujolais to kill someone? Or how was she to know where to get cyanide in the first place?

The letter ended by noting that the editors would consider a re-write if she could create a more realistic death scene.

Sagging back in her desk chair, Jana stared out her window toward Sacramento's Ella K. McClatchy Library across 22nd Street. She was unaware of the golden autumn leaves framing the historic building or of the billowing orange and yellow lantana spilling over its brick retaining wall. What use was a library that didn't even offer advice on how to poison someone?

Her trance was disrupted by the distant wailing of an ambulance. "Probably saving some life," she thought sourly.

With a sigh, she turned back to her computer screen. It must have been a lot easier in the old days when people could claim they had rats and ask the druggist how much arsenic to use. They could openly discuss the merits of cyanide versus strychnine. People weren't restricted to dropping by Taylor's Market to buy a can of Raid which came with no instructions whatsoever on the quantity fatal for a human being. How was she supposed to know how much to put in a drink? Probably a whole bottle: people were a lot bigger than ants or roaches, after all. But who'd be such a fool as to continue sipping from a cool glass of Chardonnay with a bottle of Raid in it? Or even a small amount? Wouldn't one teaspoon of Drano be so strong a person could taste it, even in the office coffee?

Pollifax, the cat, leaped gracefully onto the desk and curled possessively on Jana's open book. Jana stroked the long white whiskers, pushing them back into the orange-brown lines that patterned the shrewd little face. She wondered idly how much poison it would take to kill a cat. On that, she could experiment, although certainly not on Pollifax. Of course, cats were smart. They wouldn't lap up Drano or Raid, not even with shrimp marinated in it. Dogs, on the other hand—she listened to the neighbor's dog, Bruno, barking outside her window. Dogs were pretty stupid.

Dogs and city council members, she augmented, watching the portly figure of Councilman Garrett Melrose, the representative of her own district, climbing the steps of the library whose budget he had chipped away until now the doors opened only three afternoons a week. Where did an ordinary citizen, not a hardened felon or a drug dealer or a sleazy parolee, but just a nice, ordinary, hard working citizen, find out how much poison it took to murder Garrett Melrose? No wonder so many people were shot.

An idea was born there and then, in the quietness of an October afternoon, in a respectable apartment on a tree-shrouded street in a neighborhood with its own small public library housed in a beautiful, turn-of-the-century mansion. It was a logical idea, and a simple one, consistent with the goals and values of science: knowledge demanded experimentation.

Though she felt foolish, Jana took the precaution of shopping for poison in a variety of places, always buying a number of other items so the clerks would not get suspicious. She gradually acquired a supply of light bulbs and cat food to last her into the next century. People might look askance at a basket of sleeping pills, weed killer, roach poison, flea and tick powder, insect spray, and a varied selection of corrosive kitchen cleaners.

Not that she needed such caution. Everywhere she shopped, the clerks spoke past her to one another, apparently unable to distinguish her from a ceiling support pole.

She was in Raley's Supermarket, the big new one with so many aisles she felt safely hidden as she lingered in the cleaning supplies section, happily ensconced in the exciting reading on the back of De-Tarn Silver

Polish, when a voice reverberated in her ear.

"I use it on my badge." His voice was gentler than a late night jazz deejay, but the implications of his word "badge" were not.

She could feel the blood rush to her face. She made a point of not looking at her cart, turning instead to the speaker. She got lost in a pair of maple-syrup brown eyes, with practiced laugh creases around them, smiling down at her.

He spoke with a slow cadence, as though time were infinite. "Most people don't know our badges are sterling silver. Some officers get stainless steel so they don't have to polish them, but I kind of like to have the sterling, you know."

Warmth flooded her at his closeness. "Like—it's symbolic?" she managed.

"Yes, like that." He smiled again and tapped her bottle. "And this works very well. You have to be careful though, if you have young children around. Do you have kids?"

She shook her head no, biting back the impulse to ask if he would like to help her make some. His radio crackled, and she lost his attention as he listened carefully, then winked at her, said, "Try it," and was gone.

Well, she would try it, if he recommended it, especially since it said, in all capital letters, "Harmful or fatal when swallowed."

She did not, after all, start with the dog Bruno. It didn't seem sporting, given how much the neighbors liked him. She started, instead, with Nadine Bouvier, a co-worker with dark frizzy hair which gave her a cast like a cartoon character who had stuck her finger in an electric socket. Nadine tended to be late for meetings, to leave them early and to assume that her contribution to any committee work was to voice her opinion loudly and intractably, with no follow-through effort of any sort. Consequently, Jana often had contentious, or at least snippy, interactions with her.

As a peace offering, Jana brought a small box of chocolates and a morning cup of coffee to Nadine's desk, a tract model in the middle of a desk suburb laid out with whirring computers, clicking keys, vibrating printers, and light-blinking phones.

"Why-why, thank you," a surprised Nadine said.

Jana almost felt a little pang of remorse at how pleased Nadine looked, raising her thin turkey neck proudly up in the air so those at near desks could notice she had received a gift. But the woman's flat face scrunched up into a bitter scowl with one sip of the coffee; she didn't even swallow.

"It's definitely time," she shuddered, "for someone to clean the coffee pot."

The foul taste, however, made her eager for the chocolates, and Jana happily watched her shove two into her mouth. Jana returned to her desk and began compiling the unemployment rate by cities. She was only into the G's when Nadine yawned rudely, exposing the inside of her pink mouth and all her metal fillings to the office at large, announced that she was too sleepy to go on and promptly fell over onto her nose.

With smug satisfaction, Jana detailed Nadine's reaction in her record book. On her lunch break she made a point of stopping by Garrett Melrose's re-election headquarters, where she discovered three things: first, that he favored even more cuts in the library budget than she had heard; second, that he was the guest of honor Friday at a fund raiser for his re-election campaign; and third, that he was on a diet.

Jana trudged back toward her office, ignoring the shop windows in the downtown open mall, the latte cart that wrapped her in its aroma of coffee and chocolate, the cheerful rumble of lunch hour chitchat among bureaucrats freed for a brief respite. It was an Indian summer day blessed with gentle warmth and a clear, smog-free blue sky that curved over bright red salvia and yellow marigolds set out in huge mosaic pots throughout the downtown mall. She didn't care; she was buried in her thoughts. What was the point of giving Melrose chocolates if he was on a diet? Besides, putting someone to sleep, literally, was not at all the same as killing them. And her coffee experiment had failed; no wonder editors hadn't believed her death scenes. She was really no further along than she had been when she started.

She jumped and caught her breath as one of the increasing numbers of street people who seemed to populate her downtown area stepped into her path. Taken by that panicky feeling of not knowing what was right to do, she shoved a dollar into the outstretched hand and quickly walked into Macy's, where security guards helped customers believe in an illusory world of prosperity.

Where could the homeless man get lunch for a dollar, she wondered guiltily, and immediately felt defensive. He probably just wanted the money for alcohol.

She was passing the earring display when she halted abruptly, causing an elderly woman behind her also to stop and, in turn, to be rammed by a stroller bearing twins, both of whom began shrieking their disapproval. She heard nothing of the clamor behind her nor did she see the severe scowl on the face of the saleswoman behind the Estee Lauder counter. She saw, instead, the view in her mind, where homeless, hungry, wandering street people were metamorphosing into scientific subjects. So lost was she in her thoughts, she did not defend herself against the sample spray of Dreams Unlimited, a fragrance designed, apparently, to give wearers the impression they had just danced with a sleazy drunk who wore way too much after shave. Cheerfully, she shoved an anti-histamine into her mouth and began planning for Friday's Garrett Melrose Round Up.

On her Tuesday lunch hour she strolled into the less upscale section of downtown, daringly near a group of dirty men with ratted hair. She was approached by a gnarled, weather-beaten man about forty-five, with the weak, pale blue eyes of the very fair, carrying a hand-printed sign reading, *Will work for food. God bless you.*

"I can't give you money," she said, "but here, have a meal." She gave him a paper bag containing a sandwich, an apple, a small, personal-sized bottle of raspberry-apple juice and a little prayer pamphlet handed out by a religious group she had passed. She thought it added a nice touch.

"God bless you, ma'am."

"And you, too," she said. Crossing the street into a coffee shop, she settled by a window, sipped a mocha and watched him. As far as she could tell, the mixture of rat poison, cleaning fluid and Goo Gone she had blended into the juice had no effect whatsoever.

For her Wednesday experiment, she devised tuna salad sandwiches liberally buttered with two parts mayonnaise and one part sleeping-powder paste. The man and woman who looked like refugees from the Depression ate their sandwiches in the park, then stretched out for a nap. During her afternoon coffee break, Jana happened to catch sight of them strolling in the direction of the Loaves and Fishes shelter, looking remarkably rested.

On Thursday, she concentrated on the office coffee, having concocted a fine colorless, odorless and hopefully tasteless fluid whose primary ingredient was De-Tarn. No one in the office would do more than taste the coffee that day. As a group, they sent out to Peet's for French Roast, and the office manager put in a complaint to the building superintendent about the metallic flavor of the water in their department. Thursday night saw Jana frantically adjusting her ingredients, significantly increasing the amount of De-Tarn, but reluctant to actually taste her recipe.

She was not optimistic as she arrived for the Garrett Melrose Round Up Friday night. As she pulled into the parking lot, she realized that in her concern for the proper poison creation, she had given little consideration to witnesses. She surveyed her fellow arrivals. Even though the evening featured the currently popular country-western theme ("Lasso in the vote with Melrose"), the guests that she watched climb out of their BMWs, Mercedes and Cadillacs were not a down home crowd. These were people who wanted their roads repaired, their property protected and their taxes cut, even if libraries had to close. These were not the kind of people to shield her from police.

She entered the hall to be doubly assaulted by loud twanging music and hot, spicy chili cooking nearby, blending together in a smoky atmosphere which stung her eyes. She looked immediately for the punch bowl. The character in her book, after drinking his poisoned punch, had dropped his cup, turned bright red, spun around clutching his throat, and crashed onto the cake table.

The Melrose Round Up did not have a punch bowl; it had a no-host bar, in front of which stood Garrett Melrose himself. Melrose's relatively short body rounded in front without any indentations, like a banana. He wore a plaid cowboy shirt, a brown vest, a bolo tie, tan cowboy pants complete with scrolls on the pockets, and a belt with a silver buckle which looked as though it came from a truck stop. Lizard-skin boots held him up.

Jana rubbed the little vial of fluid in her pocket like a worry stone, watching Melrose swallow dark red liquid from his round goblet then set the glass on a table. She had poured samples of her poison into Coca-cola, coffee, Merlot, and beer. It didn't show in any of them, it didn't smell, but both she and Pollifax had declined the opportunity to taste it.

"Hi ya, there, honey, glad to see ya." Garrett Melrose's soft pink flesh pressed against her hand abruptly. "Always glad to have a pretty lady's vote." Melrose had already moved on to the next person before she could react.

Jana looked up to find her friendly police officer grinning at her. "'Always glad to have a pretty lady's vote,'" he said, and it sounded considerably more appealing than when Garrett Melrose said it.

"I didn't know officers were sent to public meetings like this," she said, wondering what to do now.

"It's private work," he answered. "We get paid by whoever hires us. We're better than security guards because we can arrest people."

And who would that be, Jana thought.

"Are you a big Melrose supporter?" he asked.

She read the name on the gold name plate above his chest pocket. D. Jameson. "What's the D for?" she asked.

He frowned, then looked down where she was looking. "Dan. And you don't have your name tag yet. They're on that table over there by the door."

"Oh."

"So what would go on it?"

It was probably unwise to give a police officer your real name when you are in the act of murder, but before she could invent some creative alternative, she heard, "Jana! What a surprise to see you! I didn't know you supported Garrett Melrose." Nadine Bouvier stood before her, dressed in a ridiculous outfit of denim skirt, red cowboy shirt, white felt cowboy hat, and vest and boots with red roses on them. "The roses are for Melrose!" she squealed. "I think that's just the cutest thing!"

"Nadine, honey, glad to see ya," said Garrett Melrose, grabbing Nadine in a big hug, his hand dangerously low on her back. "Always glad to have a pretty lady's vote."

Dan Jameson shook his head with just the tiniest sign of disapproval, nodded to Jana and made his way to the other side of the room where Jana saw another officer. Charming as Jameson was, she was pleased to see him go. She made her way to the bar, suddenly remembering that in her story a loud noise had distracted both the councilman and the witnesses so the cups could be switched. She had totally forgotten. She was woefully unprepared. However, even as she stood sipping her red wine, a solution arrived.

Eight square dancers, dressed in matching turquoise and red, with starched petticoats and sequined vests, swished in, ready to *allemande* left and right. The crowd shuffled back, squeezing from a party into an audience, their eyes on the twirling configurations, their faces recording their own discomfort, their hands clapping a rhythm for the revolving human wheel of spinning skirts and linked arms.

Poisoning the drink was even easier than Jana had written. Crushed against the broad back of a stranger, holding her glass by the stem, she lowered it in front of her, slipped the vial from her pocket and almost covered the top of the glass with her hand as she let the poison flow. Her hand above the glass was the most natural thing in the world, suggesting she didn't want to splash anyone. After a moment, she set her glass on the Melrose table to clap in rhythm with the crowd.

Then, of course, she lifted Melrose's glass, sipped and stepped back, where there was more breathing room.

She had been cool throughout, but now that it was over, heat surged through her, rolling up from her toes, seeming to reach an impasse at her lungs. A clammy sweat broke out on her hairline. She thought she could hear her heart pounding even over the throb of the amplified music beat, and she had a fearful need to visit the women's room.

But what if he sipped while she was gone? The point was not to kill him. The point was to watch him react to the poison.

Suddenly she felt nausea rising; her hands shook as she set her glass on the bar and requested a Club Soda, wishing bars served bottled Alka Seltzer.

A sudden horror jettisoned all other thoughts from her mind: what if she had picked up--had drunk from--the wrong glass? She lifted it, turning it like a connoisseur examining the bouquet and color, her mouth dry, now unconscious of any sound but her own blood pounding in her ears.

What if she had killed herself? Who would write her story? Some reporter, who interviewed some detective, who would probably claim she was feeling despair over something in her life. "If only we had known," her friends would say. "The last thing she did was to support Garrett Melrose." Probably Nadine would say that.

Even as she panicked, a wider panic charged through the crowd, disrupting the dance, curtailing the music, sparking screams and cries up through the roof. She stepped forward to watch carefully as Councilman Garrett Melrose grabbed his throat, began making choking, gasping sounds in an effort to speak and fell sideways against the broad man Jana had stood behind earlier. The two officers rushed to Melrose. Jana was not surprised that a crowd like this one turned up four doctors, each ready to administer first aid. Jameson was on his radio almost as soon as Melrose had fallen.

Despite the officers' instant demand for people to step back and give Melrose air, Jana did not comply. She stood her ground, eyes fixed on every jerking quiver of Garrett Melrose's body until it was loaded into an ambulance. She must have looked pale and weak, because Dan Jameson touched her on the sleeve and asked, "Are you okay?"

She turned with a gasp. "I-I—"

"It's very shocking, isn't it? You should go sit down."

Only then did she venture into the women's room, lock herself in a stall and record careful, detailed observations of death by poisoning.

She mailed her manuscript the first thing Saturday morning.

On a whim, after she had addressed the envelope, she also wrote a quick note to Officer Dan Jameson of the police department, referring to their earlier meeting. "In answer to your question, it's Jana Matheis," she wrote and included her phone number. She hoped he would call. She had worked so hard; she deserved a reward. She dropped the note into the mailbox, too.

MEMO. To: Jana Matheis. From: *Corpses Incorporated.*

We are returning your manuscript. Unfortunately, your story is too much like a current actual murder that occurred in your region. Our publication prefers the more imaginative approach of original fiction rather than fictionalized versions of true crime which our readers could just as well read in their newspaper. Thank you for considering us for your manuscript.

VIRGINIA KIDD is a professor emeritus of Communication Studies at California State University Sacramento. With Rick Braziel, former Sacramento police chief, she wrote *COP Talk: Essential Communication Skills for Community Policing*. She is an editor and contributor to *Memories of McClatchy Library*, a collection of stories tracing the midtown library's history, written by its patrons. She is currently finishing a full length mystery.

THE DREAM
NAN MAHON

"Watch that guy," a voice behind me said. "He'll cheat on the weight count."

I leaned forward as my bucket of grapes was lowered onto the scales, reading the count and watching the foreman write it down in my book.

"Thanks," I said to the man behind me.

"You new on the line?" he asked.

"Yeah, just got here today."

"Don't get a lot of Anglos working the fields." He was a short, muscular Mexican about my age, somewhere in his twenties. He took off his straw Western-style hat, raised his arm and wiped his face on the long sleeve of his cotton, snap-button shirt. He had a red bandanna tied around his forehead to catch the sweat that dripped from his straight black hair.

"Come from a long line of Arkansas farmers," I said. "Done this kind of work all my life."

I waited while they weighed his bucket and then stuck out my hand. "Will Harper."

"Luis Gonzales." His hand was hard and scarred, burned a dark red-brown just like his face. "I've been in the fields with my family since I was six years old. It's all I know."

The work day was over and we walked across the field. I bought a six pack of Bud from the little store up by the road. The store catered to farm hands, cashing checks, selling money orders and overpriced groceries. On pay day it did a good business with workers buying supplies for the week or sending money home through the little post office in back of the store.

Luis and I drank the beer squatting cowboy style under a big oak tree at the edge of the work camp. The grape harvest was well underway in the Sacramento Valley, and we watched the dust rise up from the road as old flatbed trucks rattled along with loads of crates. The sun cast a pink and gold smear across the sky, and we could hear children playing among the nearby cabins.

Luis and I had an easy connection, like we were cut from the same place where a need for freedom came with the DNA and living for the day seemed good enough for now.

"I did some time in the Arkansas State Pen," I told him.

"What'd you go down for?" Luis asked, tilting up the Bud can and draining the contents.

"Armed robbery. Did two years of a five year sentence."

"Parole?"

"Yeah. But I was an embarrassment to my family and couldn't get no work with a record, so I lit out."

"Jumpin' parole?"

"I 'spect they're lookin' for me." I pulled the tab of a fresh can and offered one to Luis. "But I'm just one more con on the move. Doubt they care much."

We finished off the beer and went to the camp where Luis' family offered us a plate of beans and some homemade tortillas. We sat on the porch of a cabin to eat, talking and laughing with the men. Women washed their children in the community water faucets outside the shacks and carried pails full of water inside to wash the dishes.

I had an old guitar with me, a used Gibson my daddy had got for me back when I was in high school. I could play some, those traveling Woody Guthrie kind of songs. Luis had a better voice than me and he would sing Mexican ballads about battles and towns. We started singing and other men joined in, their voices strong and full of longing for the land where they were born and loved, yet had left, looking for something better but finding instead a bitter earth and hostile people.

"You got a bedroll?" Luis asked. "Bunk in here with us. Looks like room over there in the corner."

"Kind of you," I said.

Luis had a place on the floor as did the four children. His cousin, Jose, and Jose's wife, Rosa, slept on the only mattress. No one made a fuss about going to bed, they just lay down and fell asleep in the darkness, their bodies exhausted from the day's labor.

I closed my eyes and the dream came again. The trucker in the dirty black t-shirt broke a beer bottle, slamming it on the bar so that the bottom shattered and left a splintered top half. Holding it by the neck, he came at me in a drunken rage, and I backed away until I touched the wall and there was no place to go. I pushed a bar stool between us, but he tossed it aside so that it clattered and slid across the floor. People moved away, giving room, knowing what would come next.

He was a head taller and fifty pounds heavier than me. His face glistened with sweat, and he smelled of beer and musk. By the time I got the knife out of my jeans pocket he was almost on me. I touched the button, and the blade sprang out like a flying spark. I buried it deep in his stomach, blood pouring from the wound as he staggered back, an astonished look in his eyes.

I woke up with a jerk and looked into the darkness. The room was quiet. I touched my wrists where I dreamed the handcuffs had held me, the sheriff's deputy reading me my rights in a rehearsed monotone. Turned over and went back to sleep, restless but dreamless until morning.

Life in the camp had a rhythm to it. We worked hard in the vineyards, ate simple suppers, sang in the twilight as stars popped out in a satin sky. Each night we fell into exhausted sleep in our places on the floor. In the morning, we did it all over again.

"You know," Luis told me one night as we watched light fade in the camp, the late summer evening still warm from the day's burning sun, "I've been doin' this my whole life. We pick peaches in Marysville, lettuce in Salinas and pears in the Sacramento Delta. Someday I may just hop an eighteen wheeler and keep going."

"Go where?" I asked. "To what?"

"Maybe I'll stay here when the rest move on." He raked a stick through the dirt. "I dunno."

Every man needs a friend and a plan. Luis and I were two friends looking for a direction to head into. We were young and strong with nowhere to turn, no place to go.

"Some guys join the army," Luis observed.

"Won't take me with a felony on my record."

"I don't got no papers." Luis tossed the stick away. "Let's go find Marta and Louisa, see what we can get goin'."

Sometimes in the night I awoke in a sweat. I could feel the resistance as I pushed the knife deep into the trucker's abdomen. There was blood on my hands as the deputy tightened the handcuffs on my wrists.

In the last days of summer, we all piled into Jose's old pickup and spent the day on the Sacramento River. The kids played near the bank, grabbing onto an old truck inner-tube that Jose had blown up for them. Luis and I swam nearby, keeping an eye on them in case one got in trouble with the current. Rosa went all out and made tamales for the picnic and I bought a case of beer. The weather was mild with a hint of autumn in the air and everyone felt carefree in the freedom of the day.

Luis and I sat on the bank, drinking beer and watching the kids splashing in the water while Jose took a nap under the shade of a scrub tree.

"Harvest is done here," Luis said. "We'll be movin' on soon."

I took a pull from my beer can and looked out across the river where the sun dappled the water and the children, its glare turning white everywhere it touched.

"Where you goin'?"

"Catch the last of the harvest in Oregon then on to Washington for the apples. You can come."

I was silent, watching a small branch that had broken loose from its tree ride downriver, caught in the water's rush.

"Guess not," I said.

"What'll you do?"

"Maybe head back home. I miss my family some."

Luis nodded and tossed his beer can over the heads of the children and into the river's current. It bobbed its way downstream.

Two days later, they packed up and headed north. After they left, waving good-bye from the cab of Jose's old paint-less pickup, the camper shell on back loaded with their few possessions and the kids, I felt a sting of loneliness. I had decided to go back to Arkansas and make amends with my family and my parole officer. I hitched a ride into Sacramento and walked across town to the railroad yard, hoping to find a freight that would be heading in my direction. The day was unseasonably hot, as if summer was saying a last farewell, but a cool breeze began to kick up with the evening dusk. It was a long walk with the guitar in a soft case over one shoulder and my bedroll on the other. By the time I got to the freight yard, I was pretty hot so I stopped in a beer joint near the tracks to wait for the whistle of an engine moving south, planning to jump aboard when it was too dark for the yardmen to see me.

I took a seat at the bar and ordered a beer. The girl on the stool next to me smiled and I said hello. She wore a cowboy hat over long, blond hair and jeans and a shirt with no sleeves. There was a tattoo of a coiled rattlesnake on her right shoulder.

I pointed my beer bottle in the snake's direction and said, "That's pretty menacing. Meant to keep guys away?"

"Some, I guess," she answered.

"Does it work?"

"If I want it to."

"Name's Will," I said, holding out my hand. She put hers in mine and her fingers were long and soft, the nails polished a bright scarlet.

Her eyes were deep blue and inviting, her lips red as blood.

"Cherry," she said, smiling and holding on to my hand.

Then I spotted him coming out of the men's room. He was a big man in a black t-shirt that stretched across his belly.

"You messin' with my woman, asshole," he said.

"You got it wrong, man." I dropped her hand and stood up.

He pushed in between me and Cherry, picked up my beer bottle and slammed it against the bar, busting the bottom and leaving a jagged top half.

I backed away as he came toward me. Drinkers at the bar moved, putting distance between them and the impending brawl. My back was against the wall, but he kept coming. I pushed a stool between us, but he kicked it aside. There was the smell of beer, sweat and diesel fuel on him, and a fire that I recognized blazed in his eyes. I reached into my jeans pocket and pulled out my knife, pushed the button. The blade flicked forward like a serpent's tongue, and I lunged into him.

In a flash, I remembered I had been here before, had played it all out in my dreams. But I hadn't listened to the warning so I already knew the ending.

NAN MAHON is the author of the mystery novel *Blind Buddy and Mojo's Blues Band*. Her other works include *Pink Pearls and Irish Whiskey* and *Junkyard Blues*. She is a former staff writer for *Senior Magazine*, a feature writer for *The Sacramento Bee* and the lifestyle editor for the *Elk Grove Citizen*. Nan teaches creative writing classes for the Elk Grove Unified School District Adult Education program and The Learning Exchange. A blues music fan, she is the booking agent for a local band.

GUILTY AS SIN
DENISE MARTIN

"All rise for the Honorable Chester J. Whitfield," commanded the Superior Court bailiff, calling the session to order. A tense hush filled the Placerville courtroom as all eyes turned to watch the distinguished judge enter and take his place behind the large antique desk at the front of the room.

"You may be seated," he stated matter-of-factly, as he scanned those present through squinted eyes, lowering himself into the well-worn black leather chair. Smile lines and numerous tiny wrinkles around his baby blue eyes softened the commanding presence created by his deep voice and athletic physique.

Chester "C.J." Whitfield, III was born and raised in El Dorado County, California. The first-born son of third generation cattle ranchers, he'd been expected to carry on tradition and oversee the operation of their Coloma Valley ranch. Whitfield Ranch had been in existence over 100 years and was one of few remaining cattle companies in Northern California. To his family's dismay, C.J. had chosen to pursue a law degree from McGeorge School of Law in Sacramento, leaving the ranching legacy to his younger, less prepared brother. Though many relatives were disappointed, they found it hard to criticize C.J.'s decision.

C.J. was hired directly out of law school by the Placerville law firm, Dosh, Peterson & Haynes, for whom he'd interned while attending McGeorge, and his early career ultimately benefitted the ranch while his brother did a fine job maintaining operations. C.J. eventually achieved partner status in the firm, replacing Haynes and giving a fresh start to the Law Offices of Dosh, Peterson & Whitfield. When he ran for Superior

Court judge against a long time nemesis, he did so upon a pulpit of honesty, integrity and service. He won in a landslide vote, giving credence to his "nice guys finish first" campaign slogan.

The judgeship had suited C.J. Whitfield over the years, though he was still a young forty-five. He believed in the fairness of our justice system, that a man was innocent until proven guilty and that reasonable doubt sufficiently protected the innocent. Only through some recent deep reflection on his own life did his faith in the system falter. And only then did he begin to think there might be some truth to the adage that nice guys actually finish last.

Judge Whitfield picked up black-framed reading glasses from the cluttered courtroom desk and slid them onto his nose. Then he peered over his glasses towards the jurors sitting in their assigned seats like players on a chess board waiting for the game to begin.

This unseasonably warm October day, however, he lifted the thick stack of papers in front of him and repeatedly tapped it on the desk until each corner was perfectly angled, then stared down at the tiny print on the top page, willing himself to get his head into the task at hand. The jury was scheduled to hear closing arguments in the DUI trial of a popular local bartender, but all C.J. Whitfield could think about was the horrific event that had occurred the prior weekend.

Serious crimes were a rarity in the nearby upscale town of El Dorado Hills, and the murder of a prominent local businessman-turned-politician had shocked the community to its core. The local news broke the story late Friday, and it had been the talk of the town all weekend. Certainly it had been the focus of all discussions in the courthouse this morning. The victim's ex-wife, Jennifer Hightower, was one of their very own public defenders, not to mention one of C.J. Whitfield's long-time friends.

C.J. had spoken to her briefly before trial that morning. She'd seemed shaken, but had agreed to have lunch with him at noon. He raised the sleeve of his imposing black robe to check the time on his Armitron sports watch. He was more than anxious for noon to arrive to find out what Jen knew regarding James Hightower's murder. Three hours to go, he noted. "What's three hours when you've already waited a lifetime?" he mumbled to himself. Aloud, he said, "Ladies and gentleman of the jury, today we will conclude final arguments in this trial."

Assuming Jen would not want to be bothered by staring patrons and questions from local gossips, C.J. had suggested they meet at the Mexican restaurant near the courthouse rather than the deli where they occasionally met for lunch. On arriving, he requested the more intimate table for two in the darkest corner of the restaurant. His heart quickened when he saw her enter through the large wooden doors, and the hostess directed her to their table. To him, Jen Hightower remained as deliciously beautiful as she was when they were seventeen.

C.J. stood and watched her model-like sashay as she approached. He reached out, took her hands in his and squeezed them tight, then leaned forward to place a friendly kiss on her soft, pale cheek. To his surprise and delight, she wrapped her arms around his waist and buried her face into his sturdy chest. He responded with a comforting one-armed embrace, pulling her even closer and pressing a light kiss into her golden hair. His head spun as he closed his eyes and breathed in the once-familiar smell of her, feeling the silky strands of wayward hair satisfyingly tickle his nostrils.

"You ok?" he whispered.

"I'm fine," she said. "It's been a really tough weekend."

He let her go reluctantly and pulled out a chair for her to sit, then sat himself across from her, staring at her with questioning eyes. She met his eyes and swallowed hard.

"Chelsea found him Friday when she came home from the mall. Poor thing was completely traumatized by finding her husband floating dead in their bloody swimming pool, and now Sheriff Underwood's boys are calling her one of their prime suspects, albeit among several others."

"Not to be crass," he stated, "but do you mean literally a 'bloody pool?'"

"Yes," she said, with a pained expression. "Apparently, there was blood everywhere. He'd been stabbed multiple times. Obviously, the coroner's office hasn't determined the official cause of death, but it sounds gruesome."

He reached across the table and again squeezed her hand tightly. "I'm so sorry, Jen. This must be really hard for you. I know he meant the world to you at one time. Do you think Chelsea did it?"

"Oh, come on, seriously, C.J? I mean, we all know Jim's antics could be infuriating at times, to the point many of us have said we'd like to kill him. His infidelities and indiscretions certainly caused me a lot of pain over the years. But I swear I really wanted to kill him when I heard about his latest shenanigans. C.J., he's been financially supporting young college women in exchange for sex!"

Shock briefly clouded C.J's. face before he rolled his eyes with disgust. "Really?" was all he could muster.

"And if that isn't bad enough, one of them is a local girl. His very own daughter found him out. I've been meaning to tell you about it because that local girl happens to be your daughter, Gianna's best friend! An acquaintance of Brittany made the connection a few weeks ago.

When Brittany told me about it, she said she was going to tell Chelsea. I told her she should stay out of it, but you know Brittany and her feelings towards her dad. Do I think Chelsea did it? No. I think she's a scorned wife just like I was, but I don't think she's a murderer."

There was no love lost between C.J. Whitfield and Assemblyman James Hightower, and it didn't surprise him that detectives would find multiple suspects to question. Hightower was considered a womanizing jackass by many. His shady politics had enraged people in high places throughout the region, and rumors regarding him often had been investigated in the *Mountain Democrat* and *Sacramento Bee* newspapers and local political blogs. C.J. Whitfield and James Hightower had grown up on neighboring ranches, attended the same schools and had long been fiercely competitive in sports, academics and most everything, including the pursuit of Jennifer Hightower. As had been the case often, James had won that contest. Though her friends and family had warned Jennifer against it, she'd married James soon after high school. She gave birth to their daughter, Brittany, within two years, and they were divorced before their fifth wedding anniversary.

As they finished lunch, Jen looked admiringly at C.J. "You know how much I appreciate the fact you've always been here for me. In spite of all the times you've warned me against my poor decisions, you've always been around to catch me when I fall. And you've never once said I told you so." She offered a warm smile.

"As you'll recall, Ms. Hightower, I told you back in high school that Jim would break your heart. At the same time, I told you I'd always be there for you. I meant it."

Taking advantage of the unplanned afternoon recess he'd granted following his trial's closing arguments, C.J. leisurely walked Jen back to the courthouse. As they went their respective ways, he silently chided himself for not asking her on a date as he'd wanted to do for many years. He stopped on impulse, turned back towards her and awkwardly blurted, "Hey, Jen!"

"Yes?" She turned and responded as quickly, anticipating his next question.

"Have a nice afternoon," C.J. said. "Call me if you need me."

Disappointed with himself, he meandered slowly back down Main Street to Starbucks before returning to his office. As he entered the cafe, he was surprised to see his daughter working behind the counter.

"Hi, Dad!" Gianna beamed when she saw him come through the door. She was her usual contradictory self, he observed, decked out in a cowboy-style plaid flannel shirt, jeans and boots, but flaunting long dark curls, curves and layers of make-up. Even wearing a Starbuck's apron, he thought she was the most beautiful girl on earth.

"Hey, G," he said, "I didn't expect to see you working today. I thought you were packing and loading up for your big move."

Gianna lifted the hinged counter and came running around to give him a big hug. Gianna was following in her father's footsteps and had been accepted to Hastings School of Law in San Francisco. She was planning to move in with her best friend and confidante, Clare Holm. Clare, already in her second year of law school, had graciously allowed Gianna to stay rent free in her Richmond apartment since the semester had started back in early September. Not wanting to be a perpetual freeloader, Gianna promised to move in her belongings and become a legitimate renter and roommate before the holidays.

"I wasn't scheduled to work," she told C.J., "but one of the guys called in sick. They begged me to come in and cover his shift. What can I get you, sir?" she mocked, ducking back under the counter and standing ready by the massive espresso machine.

"How about a tall, non-fat, Pumpkin Spice Latte, no whip," he rattled off.

"Coming right up, though that sounds incredibly bland." She giggled. She grabbed the tall size cup, squirted the pumpkin syrup and started the machine. "Oh, by the way, my friend, Tony, is going to help me move this weekend. You remember Tony?" She shouted over the hissing steam. "He's going to drive the U-haul and help unload, so I don't need you, after all."

An expression of severe pain crossed C.J.'s face, and he grabbed at his chest as if he had just been stabbed through the heart. "Oh, ouch, now there's a blow to an old man's ego," he exclaimed, and then he instantly felt guilty remembering Jen's description of Jim Hightower's death.

Gianna smiled up at him and as he watched her make his drink, he swelled with pride. It seemed like only yesterday that he had been jilted by Jen Hightower as a senior in high school. He had drowned his sorrow in alcohol that fateful weekend. A little too much booze and a little too much Lola Romano, and within weeks Lola was telling him that she had missed her period. Her father insisted they get married, and C.J. would have done so anyway. But it wasn't long before Lola started whining about how it was his fault that she had been forced into motherhood in a stinking one-horse town, her chances of becoming an actress ruined. She quickly left C.J. and Gianna behind to chase her dreams of a Hollywood career, only to get caught up with a third-rate producer who led her down a path to drug abuse. They had rarely heard from her since. In spite of her mother's absence, Gianna had grown up to be beautiful and smart. C.J. would do anything for her.

She handed him his latte. "Well, actually I do still need you," she said, "just not for the move. That student loan I told you about didn't pan out, so I need you to help with rent and tuition, after all. At least, until I can find a decent job."

He slipped his coffee cup into the cardboard sleeve and looked suddenly somber. "Listen, G, we've had this conversation before. I am perfectly financially capable of helping my beautiful daughter get through law school. That's not a problem. In fact, I'm glad the loan was denied so that I can help out. It's a father's right."

Taylor Swift's "Love Story" prevented her from responding as her iPhone announced an incoming call. She snatched the phone out from the large pocket of her green apron.

"Hello?"

"Hey, girlie girl." The voice was loud enough for C.J. to hear, though he could not quite make out the words. "What's up? What the hell? Did you hear about Jim? Did the cops talk to you?" The questions came at her one after another.

Gianna looked up at her father, "Dad, its Clare. I gotta take it. Talk to you later?" As he turned to walk out the door, she shouted, "Love you, Dad!"

C.J. waved a silent good-bye.

He thought about his daughter and her friend as he walked back to the courthouse. Gianna and Clare had been friends since grade school. A year apart in age, they were always together and often were referred to as two peas in a pod, though they could not have been more different. Both girls were smart, but Clare was smart like a fox, always using her wiles to manipulate people and situations to her advantage. Gianna, the more intelligent of the two, was content to be the follower. As they grew older, it occurred to him that the girls' relationship was based more on their respective needs than a true friendship. He had tried on several occasions to separate them, distracting Gianna with all manner of activities, but she would have none of them. The tumultuous friendship dance continued into junior high, high school and college. True to form, they both had applied and been accepted to Hastings School of Law. Now they shared an apartment. C.J. despaired of ever getting Gianna free.

"Did the cops talk to you?" Clare asked again into the phone.

"No, they didn't talk to me. Why would they talk to me?" Gianna said defensively. "I had nothing to do with your idiot Sugar Daddy."

"Gianna, the man's dead," Clare reprimanded. "Show a little sympathy. You told me you were thinking about signing up on Special Arrangement, so I thought maybe you had checked Jim's profile. I assume the cops are questioning anyone who contacted him through the website to request a Sugar Daddy arrangement. Did you post your profile?"

There was a long silence before Gianna responded. "No, um, well, yes, I posted a profile, briefly. And I looked at Jim's profile. I looked at other profiles, too. But I just didn't think it would work for me; the whole idea grossed me out. So I took down my profile right after I posted it. I don't need a Sugar Daddy. My real dad can help me out, at least until I find a job in the City."

Gianna recalled when Clare first mentioned her plan to seek a "Sugar Daddy" through the popular website rather than apply for a conventional student loan. Gianna hadn't known whether Clare was playing games, trying to stir up a reaction, or if she was seriously considering it. Gianna had heard about several such websites on the Oprah Winfrey show. Oprah had accused them of flat out prostitution and questioned how they could legally offer such "services" on the Web. Supporters claimed it was simply a mutually beneficial relationship providing escorts and possible intimacy in exchange for emotional and/or financial support. The fact Clare might actually consider trading sex for tuition had not surprised Gianna. Neither did it surprise her when Clare challenged her to do the same.

"Gianna, I knew you'd chicken out." Clare taunted in a witch-like cackle. "Gawd, you're so naïve, so lame."

"I did not chicken out," Gianna interrupted. "You're the one who's lame, screwing old men to pay your way through law school." Gianna's eyes began to fill with tears.

"Ok, then, maybe you didn't chicken out. Maybe Jim wouldn't have you," Clare challenged. "Maybe no one wanted an arrangement with you. No one wanted to be your Sugar Daddy. Oh, Gianna, you're a piece of work!

"And I'm not screwing old men," Clare added, "just Jim. I told you, it's a mutually beneficial arrangement. We have a mutual respect, and he really does care about me. He's been paying my tuition and my rent— rent that you've been mooching for two months. I was good with Jim. Now I'll have to find someone else and it won't be easy, you know. They're not all like Jim. You know, Gianna, if you weren't so righteous all the time, I'd think maybe you murdered Jim because he wouldn't have you!

Gianna Whitfield blinked her eyes several times to fend off the tears threatening to spill over. She had long felt inferior to Clare, though she had never understood why. She envied Clare, the bad girl, the way she always disobeyed and never got caught. The way she could drink and party without a conscience. The way she could always be the center of attention, getting any boyfriend she targeted. Gianna longed to find the courage to do something "bad" to prove that she wasn't the goody two-shoes Clare accused her of being. The truth of Clare's words stung, evoking those familiar feelings of inferiority. She was beginning to resent how Clare always mocked her. At this moment, she wasn't sure who she resented more, Clare or old man Hightower for his humiliating refusal to pay her an amount even close to what he was paying Clare.

Gianna shouted back into the phone, "No, you probably murdered Jim so he couldn't have an arrangement with me! You couldn't stand the thought that old horny Jim would have someone else to satisfy his kinky desires, someone even better than *you,* Clare!" Through blurry eyes, Gianna found and touched the End button on her iPhone, hanging up on Clare.

Weeks passed, but no arrest was made in the Hightower case. Gianna decided, at the urging of her father, to find her own apartment near the city. C.J. Whitfield could not have been happier with her decision. He paid her first month's rent and security deposit, and helped her move into the spacious studio apartment in San Pablo's Montoya Gardens. However, there was still one thing that C.J. longed for.

"Hey, gorgeous," he whispered, peeking his head into the doorway of Jen Hightower's office. "Are you available for lunch today?"

Jen immediately clicked her computer mouse to toggle to her calendar then looked quickly back at him, grinning from ear to ear. "I just so happen to be, Judge Whitfield," she replied coyly.

Happily satisfied, C.J. strolled back to his office. As he passed by his secretary's desk, he removed his wallet from the back pocket of his finely pressed gray slacks to ensure he had cash. Unfolding it, he lifted out the small business card he'd found still tucked inside: SPECIAL ARRANGEMENTS, the choice Sugar Daddy dating site for Mutually Beneficial Relationships.

He ran the card through the confidential shredder, released a heavy sigh, then smiled and returned to his desk.

DENISE MARTIN thinks there is little to like about growing old. Thus, she plans to take full advantage of what she believes are the two greatest benefits of aging: retirement and grand babies. Fortunate to retire after 32 years of State service, she plans to use her newly found freedom to rekindle her love of reading and begin her writing career. When not writing, she spends time with grandchildren, Everett and Chloe, and her two sons. Denise lives in Folsom with her husband, Tom, and their Boxer, Annie.

STIFFED
JOYCE MASON

Mr. Booze had bombed the middle of my brain. Even though I'd barely met the guy before, I knew he'd left me more than his typical calling card. I was hung over, under, around, and through. My eye teeth were throbbing.

When I'd left my office the night before, I'd had a flash intuition to ask for the next day off work because I had so much to celebrate. Then I'd sprinted the few blocks from downtown Sacramento to Old Town. Within minutes, I'd arrived at Digger's Saloon where I made happy hour look depressing compared to my elation. In no time flat, my best friend Joelle and I were toasting the arrival of my final divorce papers. I was so happy about officially ending it with Randy, I hadn't been able to wait for the weekend to celebrate.

But then was then and now was *ow*. My "personal day" had allowed me to stay bedridden past noon, the night before still a jackhammer in my head, breaking up any hope of concrete thought. I rarely drink. What could I have been I thinking?

Back to painful reality, I needed my reading glasses from my briefcase in the trunk of my car. I wanted to reread my final divorce decree and rejoice once more, this time without a chaser.

The garage felt like a mile-long walk. September heat scorched suburban Roseville, and laser-like rays glared through the garage's little diamond-shaped windows, focusing the heat with such intensity I feared something inside might combust. Or I might. I wobbled to my car and popped the trunk. My stomach lurched, and my hands came up to my mouth to hold it down. The dead man inside the trunk had had the back half his head blown off, and he didn't exactly smell like aftershave, either. There were blue-purple stains on what was left of his face like he'd been shot from behind and fell face-first into some kind of berry pie, judging by the bits of glop and pastry still stuck to him. A giggle nearly crept in, no matter how inappropriate. I felt like a little girl trying not to laugh at something goofy a friend beside her said in church. To die in pie with a purple face—

I knew those stains. After all, my ex was a berry pie junkie.

That's when it clicked. I looked past the purple face and screamed. The "DB" was my ex-husband, Randolph Dunnigan.

Randy and I hadn't exactly parted on good terms. Still, no matter how many times I might have wanted to kill him, it's not an impulse I would have ever acted on. I'd wanted to divorce him, not murder him.

This really looked bad for me.

I was too scared to call the police. Who'd believe me? I'd be the prime suspect out of several dozen with a motive to kill Randy, my ballpark estimate of the number of other women he'd taken out to the ballgame while we were still married. It had taken me a long time to know the score, even longer to know how often the scoreboard lit up. Love is blind.

"Jo?" I pleaded into my cell phone. "I need to talk to you right away, and I don't think we should do it over the phone."

"What's wrong with you, Karen? I'm in the middle of a touch-up."

"You sure sound together considering last night."

I'd known Joelle for 20 years, since we were sophomores at Del Campo High, yet I had never realized she had such a cast iron constitution. She stood on her feet all day as a hairdresser. She had to talk to people all day long—hung, strung or undone.

I whispered loudly, even though I was alone. "I just found Randy dead in the trunk of my car!"

"Oh, my God! I'll ask one of the other hairdressers to finish my client and come right over."

I could hear her shouting "family emergency" to unseen people on the salon end of the conversation. We *were* family—like sisters.

By the time Joelle arrived at my place—my former home with Randy—I had nearly paced a trench into the living room carpet. I grabbed her arm.

"Jo, what am I gonna do? You know the police will think I killed him. There's no chance I did this—is there?"

"No. No way. I walked you to the cab. We were together the whole time. Wait a minute. Who drove your car home? I wouldn't let you drive. You were too drunk. I thought you were going to leave it at work and bus back for it today. It just showed up in your garage?"

"Jo, I don't remember coming home in a cab. That's why I went to the garage. I had no idea I didn't drive home."

I stared at her, dumbfounded.

"You think you blacked out?"

I didn't know what to think. In my eagerness to put an end to my marriage to Randy, I had done something way out of character. My normal idea of drinking is a glass of wine with dinner at a nice restaurant, a few times a year.

As if reading my thoughts, Joelle said, "You're five-four, too little to lift a 200-pound man into a car trunk. I don't know how the police could like you for this. Was it a knife or gun? Or—?"

"I think you'd better see for yourself."

Joelle shivered. Goose bumps popped, but I knew she could stomach anything. She had practice from listening to the gory gossip at the hair salon.

I led Jo into the garage, temporarily forgetting about the blueberry face till Joelle took one look at the late Randy Dunnigan. I heard her initial gasp morph quickly into what sounded like nervous laughter.

"Looks like he got the old comedy pie in the face!" Jo said.

I wondered aloud if he'd been eating in or out. "Berry pie was his fave. Could have gone either way. He always kept a Marie Callender's in the freezer."

We laughed till we hugged.

"We'd better go inside and figure out what to do," Joelle advised.

I had made some coffee to help me sober up further, although I have to say, finding Randy dead in my trunk had pretty much done the trick. Jo and I sat down, sighed a lot, and drank our coffee in silence for some time before she offered an idea. Thank God, because I was still brain dead.

"Look, Karen. We need to be armchair detectives. We need to figure out who else may have had a reason to kill Randy."

"I can name about 36-24-35 of 'em," I said.

"An angry lover would be a rage killing in the moment. This looks premeditated. He was eating—probably taken by surprise from behind. We need to find out who would *benefit* from Randy's death."

At first, I just wanted to write off Jo's habit of analyzing everything as high drama from watching too many crime shows. Yet, she had a point. Unfortunately, the facts on the subject didn't make me look any better. I was still the beneficiary of Randy's life insurance policy. Under the terms of the divorce, I would remain so for as long as he was court-ordered to pay me alimony. That was for the next five years. My lawyer had felt the insurance policy would guarantee that I'd get a reasonable window of time for economic transition and the resources needed to reconstruct my life if Randy died. Who knew it would ever turn out to be anything more than a big, unlikely what-if?

When I explained all this to Joelle, she had another question that proved she was thinking a lot more clearly than I was.

"If you were out of the picture, like if you died or went to jail, who'd get his insurance? By the way, how much is it?"

I almost choked on the words.

"It's a million."

"A million? That's unbelievable! You're rich! Someone may have just done you a huge favor."

I didn't see it that way. My marriage to Randy was a disaster, but I'd never wished him dead. Benefitting from Randy's or anyone's death was the last thing I wanted. But I had to admit, the money—assuming I didn't spend the rest of my life in prison falsely accused of murder—would make things a lot easier. My self-esteem was in the cellar after Randy's playing around, and it would be nice to salve my wounds and build myself back up on some tropical island with a spa and a lot of hunky men flirting with me, a rich American "widow."

"His brother, Jeff, is the next in line as beneficiary," I said. "He's all the family Randy had left, and he's single."

The idea of Jeff offing his only brother didn't ring remotely possible. I liked Jeff. He'd been a good brother-in-law.

Despite my protests, Joelle suggested I look at this in a more calculated, detached manner, the way the police would look at it. No possible suspect could be discounted.

"Not even you," I said to Jo, a wry reference to the time she had once succumbed to Randy's charms herself.

"I thought you'd forgiven me that one indiscretion. Alcohol and other mood-altering substances were involved and, don't forget, you were separated at the time."

"Just being thorough," I said. If I'd been writing it, I'd have typed LOL. I *had* forgiven her.

I had an alibi all night until Jo saw me into the cab. No one could vouch for me past being dropped off at home. I felt doomed.

"Will you visit me in jail?"

Jo wasn't laughing.

"Look, Karen. We have to call the cops. We can point out that anyone as ripped as you were would be too out of it to drive home, much less kill a big man and stuff him into the trunk. I put you in the cab and could probably identify the driver. Funny looking guy. Reminded me of Steve Buscemi in *Fargo*."

I sure hoped I had tipped that cab driver.

I trembled calling 911. My nerves had me one jump ahead of a fit between the emergency call and the time the sirens and flashing lights started closing in. Little did I know then that the cops and their investigation would up-end my life even more than my dead ex-husband, Randy Dunnigan, with his face full of pie.

The cops I got weren't bad. They reminded me of Danny Reagan and his partner, Jackie Curatola, on the TV show, "Blue Bloods." "Danny" was fortyish with dark, close-cropped hair. Like the TV Danny, he was a volatile cynic. His real name was Mick Clegg. "Jackie" was Olivia Ortiz, whose parents apparently liked alliterations, though I heard Clegg call her Livvy. She had long, dark hair pulled back in a ponytail and no wedding rings. She exuded both warmth and authority, which I admired as a tough combination to pull off.

After gathering all the facts, with Joelle elaborating certain scenes and providing my alibi, the detectives looked up when a third man, a CSI, brought a report from my garage.

"It wasn't hotwired," CSI Scott Hampton reported. "No locks picked. Someone had to have the key and probably the remote. 'Else how did they get into the locked garage?"

The only other person who had ever had a set of keys and remote to my vehicle was Randy. Like most couples, we sometimes switched cars for one reason or another. Randy drove a Beemer, so he only used my Toyota when he had something grungy to carry (thanks) or his BMW was in the repair shop. I thought I had gotten the keys back from him when we separated but, quite honestly, I couldn't say for certain. It was a time of yelling and drama.

Scott-the-CSI also reported that the guy from the County Coroner's Office, still poking at Randy's dead body, had made a preliminary estimate of the time of death: noon Wednesday.

"Where were you yesterday afternoon?" Detective Ortiz asked me.

"At work the whole time." I had dozens of witnesses.

Clegg registered what I'd said. "The ex is always a person of interest, especially when the husband ends up dead in her car. But to tell the truth, as long as your alibi checks out, from what I get here, it wouldn't have been possible for you to kill him, even if the time of death turns out to be later on a closer look. You were too blasted to do it after you left work, and you're too small to pull off moving his body."

Joelle beamed.

"If you don't have another set of keys and remote to your car, I think we've got to assume that the spare set came from the victim," Clegg said.

Joelle frowned. "You gave me a set, in case of emergency."

Apparently I'd forgotten.

"Where do you keep them?" Ortiz asked.

Joelle rose, got her purse and started digging. She held up the keys.

"Thank you," Detective Clegg said. "That still leaves the possibility that the victim kept his set, and someone took them and used them directly or made copies. For now, just go about your life. We'll be in touch. Don't leave town."

Go about my life? Yeah, sure.

I could tell no one at work believed I'd done it because they asked me a million questions. If they'd thought I was guilty, they'd have been quiet, walking on eggs, making me feel uncomfortable. Instead, I'd become the most exciting subject at our public relations firm since we'd pitched rebuilding the image of our philandering ex-governor.

My colleagues' enthusiastic support and belief in me didn't make me feel much better, however. I went back to work the following Monday— early, all things considered. Truth is I'd never hated Randy; I'd just hated our sham marriage and the pain his dishonesty caused me. I was genuinely sorry he was dead.

Meanwhile, I talked with Randy's brother Jeff about making arrangements, once Randy's body was released. Apparently, Jeff believed me, too. He also figured I knew better than anyone what Randy would have wanted, having lived with him the longest and most recently, nearly 14 years. Jeff and I agreed easily: cremation, no formal service and a memorial gathering with an open bar. That's what Randy always talked about: more of a party. I braced myself for a long line of his women to show up.

Sadness set in once I felt confident I wouldn't be falsely imprisoned and sent to Death Row. My nights were tearful and miserable as I wondered what I could have done differently to make the last year of Randy's life better for both of us.

When the cops didn't report any progress on finding his killer after a week, I contacted the insurance company to discuss initiating my claim. The pot was so big, I planned to offer Jeff half of it or whatever amount he felt comfortable taking. I didn't need a million dollars, even if it would have been nice. A half-million was plenty and, to be honest, it was partly my way of making something up to Randy for being such a bitch at times. Jeff would have gotten it all if we had been outside the five-year period after the divorce and I would have gotten zip, so it seemed right to me to split it. I was waiting for the best time to bring it up. Jeff was so bereaved, he hadn't even asked about the insurance. He just asked me if I needed his help to cover any of Randy's final expenses.

Randy had joked that he wouldn't tell Jeff he was on the life insurance, in case his brother had any hidden Cain and Abel tendencies. Apparently, he hadn't been kidding about not telling him... unless Jeff was just playing dumb...

Nah.

Truth is I wasn't ready yet to tell Jeff that while Randy had stiffed me out of a faithful marriage, I was flush when it came to insurance. Jeff offered to help me. I wanted to help him.

Week Two after the murder brought a phone call and request for some preliminary paperwork by Randy's insurance company. While the investigation continued, the death certificate was issued, so we could move forward. Apparently, the police had informed the insurance agent, a bleached blonde named Laurette Enwright, that I was no longer a person of interest in Randy's murder. She knew more than I did. I'd called Detective Ortiz numerous times for updates, and she had always given me the same line, "We're working on it. I'll call you when there's a break in the case."

Laurette met me in my office on a Tuesday afternoon. Wearing a scandalously short skirt, she teetered on four-inch stilettos. She also wore way too much make-up. It made her look older, not younger which, I assumed, was her intention. Laurette looked more like one of Randy's girlfriends than his insurance agent, a profession I used to consider conservative. Something about her bothered me, even more than her oozing pheromones.

"Big policy," Laurette said. "Not often you see a guy leave a million dollars to his ex when there are no kids involved."

"Randy's software company was likely to make us rich one day, and he wanted me to be provided for."

He was more than willing to agree to alimony and keeping me on his insurance for five years. Randy had a lot of guilt. He loved me, even if our ideas of marriage differed drastically.

"Then there's the double-header."

"What do you mean?"

"Dooley, Randy's business partner in Dunnigan & Dooley. Randy had another policy for a million on his life with Dooley as his beneficiary. It's very common among business partners, so that one guy's not left holding the bag for money or brain trust if the other dies first. You didn't know?"

"Not a clue," I said, wondering if Detectives Clegg and Ortiz knew this compelling fact. I couldn't wait till Laurette left to call Livvy Ortiz who merely said "very interesting," during our two-minute conversation.

On Friday, Week Three, I got a call from Joelle a lot like the one I'd made to her three weeks earlier.

"Karen, I'm in trouble. I need you to come down to the police station *now*. I've been arrested. I can't give you the details over the phone. You're my one call. Bring your lawyer's card so he can refer us to a criminal lawyer. Ask for Clegg and Ortiz when you get here."

She clicked off. Criminal lawyer. Clegg and Ortiz?

I was shaking when I got there and asked for the detectives. What about Dooley? He was the one who stood to benefit from Randy's death. Why was Jo arrested? Nothing made sense.

The detective duo escorted me into a private interview room. "You can see Joelle after we talk to you," Livvy Ortiz said. "That is, if you still want to."

Mick Clegg didn't beat around the bush. "Your BFF whacked your ex."

Reeling, I countered, "But that doesn't make any sense whatsoever. Why would she do that?"

Ortiz: "Jealousy and rage is my guess."

"What?"

"First off," Clegg said, "she has no alibi during the day of the murder. She took the day off work. Second, she had keys and access to your car and knew you had temporarily abandoned it. She also knew you'd be passed out and wouldn't hear her drive it into your garage in the wee hours of the morning. Third, we got a search warrant for her place and found a gun that matches ballistics for the murder weapon."

Joelle? A murderer?

"That is not the Jo I know. I just can't imagine this is true."

"Talk to her yourself," Ortiz suggested. "She doesn't deny it, but she lawyered up."

Jo looked dumpy for a girl in the glamour business. Her shoulders slumped and her entire demeanor sagged. She raised her head when I entered the interrogation room.

"Jo, what is this?" I asked.

Her moist eyes flashed. "I'm done lying to you, Karen. There was more than one night between Randy and me. I hated myself for it, but I also couldn't help it. Randy was like a drug to me. But when he made it clear that your divorce would make no difference to my status with him, I realized he'd used me like all the others. I'd been foolish enough to think that after a while I could come clean with you, and Randy'd marry me. I thought maybe you'd even be OK with it, eventually. You forgave me once. Maybe you'd forgive me for all of it."

I wanted to cover my ears and sing a loud *la-la-la* like I had when I was a kid and couldn't stand to hear my parents argue. I wanted to block out everything Jo was saying.

"He used us both," she continued. "I couldn't contain my anger any longer. I had to do something about it. I also wanted you to get the money. One of us deserved to get something out of the bastard. I was hoping you'd take me on at least one good vacation with you."

"But you didn't know about the insurance till I told you," I said.

"I lied about that, too. Laurette Enwright is a client of mine. She let it slip one day. She asked me about that picture of us from high school on my station at the salon. She asked me who you were. Dunnigan was a familiar name to her. It was weird that she handled Randy's policies, and, to tell you the truth, I suspect she handled him, too."

Jo was bigger and stronger than I was, both physically and emotionally. I know it's wrong, but I had to stifle a laugh when she told me she'd used a dolly to move Randy into his own garage for storage, wheeling him like so many cartons till she could retrieve my car and stuff him in it. I soon sobered.

"How could you put Randy in my trunk? How could you implicate me like that?"

"I knew you were too squeaky clean for it to stick. I figured they'd suspect Dooley, once they knew he had a million to gain and could probably access Randy's set of your car keys. I knew Randy still had a set. He'd mentioned needing to return them to you. Besides, I'd seen them in plain sight on a hook in his kitchen. Couldn't miss that distinct shape of your remote. I figured if the cops thought you'd given me my own set, I'd seem trustworthy. Same with openly admitting I had them."

That had sure backfired.

I couldn't resist asking Jo, "Couldn't you wait till he was done with dessert?"

"Bad timing, I know, but an irresistible pun and poetic justice. After all, when it came to loyalty, he'd deserted us both."

Even after all she'd done, I missed Jo at Randy's memorial, which was actually the most fun I've ever had at a "funeral." Jeff was great, especially back at my house after everyone was gone and the dust had settled on Randy Dunnigan's final farewell. I didn't drink nearly as much as I had the night I celebrated my divorce, but there was one last drink that was really memorable.

Over a glass of wine, I offered Jeff half of Randy's insurance money.

"There's actually something else of Randy's I've always wanted," he said.

Jeff put his hand over mine.

JOYCE MASON is a prolific writer and professional astrologer. She has published three ebooks on astrology, articles in astrology journals worldwide, and a small short story collection. Her blog, "The Radical Virgo" (www.radicalvirgo.com), features half of the 400 articles she has written on her own and others' blogs. Her story "Digital" appeared in the 2008 *Capital Crimes* anthology. Two more books are lined up for publications: a new astrology book and her first mystery novel, *The Crystal Ball*. Joyce and her husband, Tim, reunited childhood sweethearts, live with their fur family in Rocklin. Visit her at www.JoyceMason.com.

MURDER INTERRUPTED ME
PATRICIA L. MORIN

I have waited for this day forever. Well, yeah, at least it seems that way. Like eons, man.

My wife rarely gives me time I can call my own. I'd say seconds, but that would be too long. I'd say nanoseconds, but you know what? The shit I take makes time meaningless. Just like my life is meaningless to my old lady.

How I've longed for this day! To finally unwind, fish, do drugs in the open air and, most important, be alone. Oh, yeah. I love being alone. I love alone. Sitting here next to the stream, fishing, tripping, toking, just me, myself, and I. Heaven! Though on this shit, you're never really alone.

Still, you know what I mean. Without the bitch hounding, hounding me—"Mow the lawn!" "Clean the garage!" "Fix the leaky faucet!"—I get to see the deep, rippling stream yanking at my feet, like it wants to grab them. I get to hear the rushing water and the air rustling through the long soft grass, like fingers fluffing hair, but louder. Hell, I get to focus on one blade of grass, become it and feel the heartbeat of nature pounding in my chest.

Wow, am I buzzing. Shoulda taken a little less.

Then again, maybe not. I mean, I'm sitting on the bank and hanging over it in the sky. I scan Earth through my telescopic vision, courtesy of my best girlfriend, Mary Jane, and Ice, cold blue and fast, and two tasty blotters of acid, purple Popeyes painted on them. Can you feel it, too? Are you getting a contact high? Oh, man, it's the most wonderful place to be in the universe, and I mean the whole wide world, from Spain to

Austral... ya... Aus... Oz! Yeah, man, that way big continent in... like... the ocean. The ocean. Ocean big. All that water. This water, in this stream, eventually finding its way to that water, in that ocean.... .

Where was I?

Oh, yeah, puffing, puffing, puffing along with Mary Jane. Yeah. Puff the plastic decoy lived by the stream and frolicked in a—

"What the hell are you doing!"

Hm. Is that noise inside or outside my head? Has to be inside, seeing as how my head is the universe.

I turn around, which takes a really long time, but finally I look and I see... boots. Workman's boots. I think. I mean, the shape I'm in, I can't be sure. Because they also resemble puppies, with big noses in front and all the little eyes making two big eyes, though they need floppy ears hanging over each side, maybe skimming the ground. If one puppy went to bite the other puppy's ear, would the big workman trip and fall on his face? Too funny.

"What are you laughing at? This is my land and you're trespassing. I'll give you ten seconds to leave. Then I'm calling the police."

Ten seconds? How long is that? Oh. Yeah. About as long as my wife gives me to think about what I want to do and not what she wants me to do. Oh! Wow! That cloud over his shoulder. Is it the face of a woman screaming? Her mouth is getting wider and wider and wider. She must be screaming louder. There isn't a day goes by that I don't hear screaming. My wife screaming how unhappy she is. Screaming like the cloud.

Man, this dude is big. Towering over me. Should probably get up and talk to him, face to face, although I can't make out his face. Where is his face? Sun's too bright!

The puppies are glaring at me. The two metal eyes and the long nose held together by string. No, no, rope. No, no, shoelaces, no, rope, no, string. The sole is separating and mouth is opening, ready to scream at me. Like the cloud. The other puppy is looking on.

"Bite that other puppy's ear," I say to the quiet one.

"You're fuckin' stoned!" The faceless voice yells down at me. "You're out-of-it. Can you even think straight? You were smoking pot, weren't you? I know you were."

"This is California. Stoned is okay. I have my medical card." I shove my hand into my pocket and search for the card. Not there. Other pocket. I go to the other pocket and slowly pull it out. "Look."

"You're not just stoned! You on other drugs? Do you even know where you are?"

"Shoot, yeah. Hell, yeah. South Fork somewhere, Folsom Lake, Folsom, Folsom... prisons and dams. Ha! Damn prisons... ha... ha...

ha." I start singing, "I walk the line, ha... ha... ha. Me and Johnny."

"I'm trying to help you stay out of prison! You're trespassing. You better get out of here, right now."

"Right this nanosecond?" I laugh.

The screaming cloud distorts. The mouth separates and disappears.

"That's your Celica parked right out there on the road, isn't it?" He points to the road behind me.

"Yep."

"For the last time and for your own good, I'm telling you to leave. Otherwise, you're going to be in big trouble."

"Okay." The puppies are smiling at me now. Quiet puppies. Good puppies.

"Okay? Okay what? Get up and leave!"

"Okay, you're telling me for the last... Hmm..."

The one puppy opens its mouth. "That's it! I'm calling the cops."

The puppy's a riot.

"It's not funny. Get up!"

"Okay, puppy, I'm moving." I figure I should anyway. The cops and all. I bend my legs and push. "I'm moving, see? You're as mad as my wife on Saturday morning."

"Huh?"

"She gives me a big fuckin' list of chores. No fishing. Just yelling. No talking like we used to. No asking. Big list to keep me away. Now I'm away."

He shakes his head.

I get up. I'm up. I watch the current trying to grab my feet. I stomp on it. It spits at me.

"So, you're not too fucked up to move. Good. Now go."

I look and the huge guy without a face is now wearing bottle-thick glasses, staring at me. The better to see you with, my dear? The big brown eyes, the color of dead leaves, blink. Those glasses, I think, like microscopes.

"Go ahead. Call the cops," I say as I stumble toward the stream. "But I gotta move this log. Can't fish with this log in the way."

"What log? What fish?"

I glance back at the guy. Now he doesn't seem that big. He's not reaching for his cell phone. He's not moving at all. At least, I don't think he is. But the puppies are staring down the road, like they hear something coming. And his hands have turned into claws, big rounded hooks that could tear me apart.

Wow. Maybe I shouldn't have had that second acid blotter.

Jesus, that's a big log for such a small stream. Seems stuck. If I move it, I'll bet there's a big-ass fish lurking underneath.

Ah, fishing! Finally. How long has it been since I went fishing? Can't even begin to remember. At least since I got married. She was so nice before that. But then she—

Fuck it! Just fish! See the water separate, no flapping. Listen to your breathing like the current. Smell the dirt. Feel the freedom as you reel it in.

"Rick, you gotta get the fuck out of here now!" he yells. "Otherwise, it'll be too late. Leave now!"

Too late? For what? Dinner? To ride the sky? And how does this guy know my name?

He's still talking. At least, his mouth is moving. But now I can see through him. Like the dirt, grassy shit, yeah, right through him.

And look. The log is moving toward me. I see the trees. Breeze smells funny now. I feel the water at my feet. I hear wheels on gravel.

The sun's rays tap the water, causing little ringlets to appear next to one another. The fish bites. Lucky me. My little fly decoy caught a big-ass fish right near the log.

"Run!" he screams. "Run now! Right now!" He slowly rises from the earth, like a slow-moving helium balloon, the puppies reaching my knees, then my shoulders, and finally my face. They stare at me, their ears limp, their eyes dead. One of them opens its mouth to say, "I tried to warn you, Rick. I tried. That's all a survival instinct can do. But you wouldn't listen. You're too fucked up to know it's me, your survival instinct. Run!"

Something stirs deep inside me. My stomach hurts. That's all a survival instinct can do? Not a real guy, a survival instinct? But then I laugh it off. Ha ha! Funny, those puppies.

A pointed triangle pops out of the water, a small pointed triangle, with nostrils.

This is very strange. Fish don't have nostrils, do they?

Strong shit. Woo.

The current's really ripping. It will help pull in the fish.

Oh, there's the mouth, open wide like in a circle. A car door slams behind me. I turn and see flashing lights and a man in uniform talking into a box that crackles. Another man holds a photo.

I like my puppies better.

"He's here."

True enough. I am here.

A man walks over to the edge of the stream and looks at a photo in his hand. "Yep, that's her."

Yeah, big-mouth bass, I think. On the log? No.

The man with the photo looks at me and says, "You're under arrest for the murder of your wife."

Someone else grabs me and pulls my arms behind my back.

"I am? No, man, I was just fishing."

"Fishing? You don't even have a fishing rod!"

Pat Morin's short story "Murder Interrupted Me" won the Summer 2013 Mill Valley Literary Magazine Contest" and was published in the e-magazine in October 2013.

PATRICIA L. MORIN, a psychotherapist with masters degrees in both Counseling Psychology and Clinical Social Work, writes short stories, novels and plays. Her first short story collection, *Mystery Montage*, was released by Top Publications Ltd., Dallas TX, in 2010. The story, "Homeless," was a Derringer and Anthony award finalist, while "Pa and the Pigeon Man" was nominated for a Pushcart. Her second short story collection, *Crime Montage*, was released by Top in March 2012. A third collection will be released by Harper Davis Publishing Co., CA, in 2014. To learn more about Patricia L. Morin and her work, visit her at www.PatriciaLMorin.com.

BAD NEWS IS GOOD NEWS
KAREN A. PHILLIPS

Saturday morning dawned with nothing new to investigate or report. No car accidents, no wives wanting evidence on their cheating husbands, no dead bodies. Nada. Zilch. Jennifer and Max sat in a historic brick building turned coffee shop near Old Town Sacramento. As the sun rose, they sipped lattes while commiserating on their shared misfortune. The sweet taste of their favorite beverage did little to lighten the mood.

"I'm telling you, Max," Jennifer said, "things have gone from bad to worse." She held up her thumb and forefinger. "I'm this close to declaring bankruptcy. The Cap City Detective Agency may have to close its doors.

"Honey, I had no idea it was that bad." Max shook his head. "It's this damn economy. Why do you think they call it the Great Recession? Sam and I are having to eat *in*, for God sakes."

"Funny," Jennifer said to her best friend. She looked out the window beside them. Outside, the world appeared bright and sunny, another beautiful day in California. Early risers strolled past, going about their lives, unaware of Jennifer's misery. She turned her attention back to Max, leaning in close as if to share a deep, dark secret and looked into his blue eyes.

"Max," she whispered, "I'm thinking of killing someone just to get the work."

Max choked on his coffee, sending a splash of brown liquid down the front of his blue shirt. He grabbed hold of the chair as a coughing fit overtook him.

An employee suddenly appeared, thrusting napkins at Max. "Sir, are you okay?"

Max waved her away with a limp napkin. "She just tried to kill me, but luckily her attempts were thwarted."

Jennifer barked out a laugh. "Don't listen to him. He's a newspaper reporter. He'll do anything for a story."

The girl looked at them as if they were crazy and left.

"You're wicked," Max said.

They started laughing, causing Max to cough in earnest.

"Well," Max said, drying his eyes with the sleeve of his shirt, "now that the fun and games are over, anything new with Tabitha?"

"Just typical surly-teenager stuff," Jennifer said, checking her watch. "Since school let out, she's been sleeping in."

"Oh, yes. She's turning thirteen this year. Sam and I will plan something special for her. Maybe take her to the beach. Work on my tan for the summer."

"She'd love that," said Jennifer.

"And how's the ex? Still with that sketch artist he dumped you for?"

Excuse me, 'forensic artist,' according to her. Yes. He's still with her. Do I detect a note of old man cynicism?"

"I must admit I've been feeling my age," Max said. "The fabulous forties are not all that fabulous." He ran a hand through his short, blond hair flecked with grey. "Do you think my hair is thinning?"

Jennifer rolled her eyes, then noticed that the clothes he wore hung loose on his athletic frame. "Have you lost weight?"

"Yeah. It's called the 'anxiety diet.' It's all the rage, but I don't recommend it."

"Enough with the jokes, funny man. What's really going on?"

Max's shoulders slumped as if Jennifer had stuck him with a pin. "It's Sam."

She touched his hand. "Is he okay?"

"Oh, he's fine. It's me that's not. I think he's seeing someone." Jennifer observed her handsome friend. "I feel bad," she said. "Here I am going on about my problems. What makes you think that about Sam?"

Max reached for his leather jacket and pulled a swath of gold fabric from a pocket, but before he could explain, his cell phone rang to the tune of "You Ain't Nothin' But A Hound Dog."

"Max here."

Jennifer saw his body tense. After the call, he stood up, slid the phone into his pants pocket and looked at her with an unreadable expression.

"Mom always said 'be careful what you wish for, darlin','" he said in a somber tone. "Dead body found in Capitol Park." He grabbed his jacket.

"I'm right behind you," Jennifer said, just as her cell phone rang. "Mom? When are you coming home?"

Jennifer opened the door to the cramped townhouse she shared with her daughter and threw her purse on the dining table where it toppled to the ground. She pinched the bridge of her nose and stared at the lump of black leather as if it symbolized everything wrong in her life. Max wasn't answering her calls. She struggled between wishing she had followed him to the crime scene and needing to get home to her daughter. Dead bodies were her business, and she desperately needed the work. She dreaded having to close her office and get a regular job.

But her daughter was also her business. Motherhood and detective work didn't always mix well, but Jennifer tried her best.

The subject of her thoughts sat at the computer in an alcove off the kitchen.

"Hi, Mom," Tabitha said with a quick wave, her attention never leaving the computer.

Jennifer scanned the kitchen for evidence of food preparation and detected that her daughter had not eaten yet. Jennifer sighed audibly, grabbed her cell phone from her purse and tried Max again, but got voice mail once more. "Max, call me," was all she said.

"How is Max?" Tabitha asked, finally turning around.

"Tabitha Marie!" Jennifer shouted. "What is that on your face?"

Tabitha pointed to her lips. "The black lipstick?" she asked innocently. "Isn't it cool? All my drama friends wear it."

"Is that so?"

"Mom, my Facebook page says I'm a witch in our school play. I'm just having fun with the role."

With her pale skin and straight black hair, Tabitha already looked the part.

"Young lady," Jennifer said, throwing her a roll of paper towels, "you will wipe that off your face. This isn't your drama class. This is real life. And how many times have I told you to be careful what you post on Facebook?"

"Don't worry, Mom."

"Tabitha, there are bad people out there—"

"Waiting to take advantage," Tabitha finished for her. "I know. I know." She rolled her eyes.

"I make a living investigating those same people. You have no idea how bad they can be."abitha got up and walked into the kitchen. "When are you going to let me help you with your investigations, Mom? I'm old enough to be your assistant."

Jennifer opened the refrigerator and pulled out a carton of eggs. "I think you're old enough to help me make breakfast," she said, tossing a loaf of bread to Tabitha.

"I'm not a kid anymore."

"You remind me on a daily basis, honey."

Jennifer's cell phone rang.

"Max?"

"No, this is Rosie, your mother. Remember me?"

"Hi, Mom. How are you?"

"I'm fine, dear. But I know you need some work and I've decided to hire you."

"Mom, if you're trying to humor me, I'm not in the mood."

"I'm serious. I want you to investigate Abner. I thought after your father died that I was ready to date, but now I think I made a mistake."

"The man is ten years younger than you," said Jennifer. "I've always wondered about that."

"Yes, dear," Rosie said. "Anyway, I showed him my letter from Leland Stanford to President Lincoln, and he got very excited about it. Said it was worth a lot of money. He wanted to sell it at auction. When I said no, he got so mad I hardly recognized him."

Jennifer felt a spark of anger catch in her belly. "Did he hurt you, Mom?"

"Well, I do have bruises where he grabbed my arm. He said he was sorry. But now it's missing."

"The letter? Are you sure?"

Jennifer's cell phone beeped an incoming call.

"Mom? Hold on. Pete's calling." She hit the connect button. "What's up?"

"Jen. There's been a murder," her ex-husband said. "I'm at the scene now. Max was just here. He looked like he'd seen a ghost."

Jennifer's heart skipped a beat. "Just a sec, Pete." Jennifer held the phone to her chest and snapped her fingers to get Tabitha's attention. "Check *The Sacramento Bee* website and see if Max posted anything about a murder."

Tabitha gave her a thumbs up and headed to the computer.

"Okay. What can you tell me?"

"The vic's name is Sam Dansforth."

Jennifer gasped. Max's partner! The news caught her by surprise, raising her detective hackles.

"What is it, Jen? Did this guy owe you money?" Pete asked, laughing. "Sorry. Bad joke."

"I'm not laughing. Sam is, or was, Max's partner."

"No shit? Now his behavior makes sense. How well did you know Sam?"

"Not well, but they seemed happy. Until recently."

"Oh?" Pete asked in his cop voice. "Tell me."

"Let's trade information. What can you tell me about the crime scene?"

For a minute, Pete didn't answer and Jennifer could hear voices in the background and someone saying, "Move along folks."

"Okay. What I told Max I can tell you, but it's off the record."

"You know you can trust him."

"That was before I knew him as suspect number one," Pete said. "We found tire marks on the scene."

"Car tire marks? In the park?"

"Not a car, smaller. We got a cast of the tread pattern. We're looking into it. I'll get back to you on that."

"Which reminds me, Pete. When will I get the child support check?"

"How 'bout I drop it by tonight and you can tell me what you know. Plus, I'll spend some time with Tabitha. I promise."

"Stop promising. Just do it."

When she hit the connect button to talk to her mother, she was gone. Jennifer tried calling back, but the phone rang until she gave up.

"Anything on *The Bee*'s site?" she asked Tabitha.

Tabitha turned from the computer, her eyes as big as her open mouth.

"What is it?" Jennifer said, rushing to her side.

"Poor Max," was all Tabitha could say.

Jennifer looked her daughter in the eye. "You really want to be my assistant?"

"You know I do!"

"Then you start now," said Jennifer. "Let's go." She grabbed her purse and they headed to the garage.

They parked in front of a building directly across the street from the state Capitol and Capitol Park. How convenient, Jennifer thought. Above the door was a black canvas awning bearing the outline of a crown over the name of the shop: "Royal Antiques & Auction House" in white lettering. In one window, a neon sign flashed "OPEN" in red.

"Let's do some detecting, Nancy Drew," Jennifer said to Tabitha.

"Who?"

Jennifer opened the car door. "Google her."

Mother and daughter stood side by side on the sidewalk. They had discussed a plan on the drive over.

"You ready, Watson?" Jennifer asked.

"Okay, Mom, stop with the names. Yes. I'm ready."

They opened the front door and heard the tinkling of a bell announce their arrival. A combination of smells greeted them, the sharp scent of cleaning polish mixed with a redolence of old buildings and damp spaces. A bespectacled man wheeled a dolly full of cardboard boxes into a side room. He returned moments later and stood behind a glass display cabinet where a long sword lay next to rags and a can of polishing solution.

"Good afternoon, ladies," he said. "May I help you?"

Tabitha walked up to the counter, the bare wooden floor creaking under each step.

"What kind of sword is that?"

He waved the sword in the air, and the bright metal flashed in the light.

"It's a Spanish sword used in the English civil war. Very rare."

"Speaking of rare," said Jennifer, "do you have any rare documents for sale?"

The man looked at Jennifer as if assessing her value. "What, specifically, are you interested in?"

"Something from the old railroad days, for instance."

"I'm doing a project in school," said Tabitha.

The man looked perplexed. "I don't understand. A school project involving rare documents?"

"My daughter wants to use something unique," Jennifer said with a smile.

"Yeah. Like everyone else just copies stuff off Google or Wikipedia," said Tabitha, giving her best eye roll. "That's so, you know, lame."

The man's eyes twinkled. "I think I have just the thing." He raised a finger. "Wait right here. I'll just be minute." He opened a side door and disappeared, shutting it firmly after him.

Tabitha looked up at her mother and grinned. "High five, Mom," she whispered, holding up her hand.

Jennifer quietly slapped her palm and grinned back.

The door opened and they looked over expectantly as the man stepped back into the room with a black leather case. He spread a black cloth on top of the counter and carefully placed the case on it. The shape of a crown, matching the crown on the awning, was embossed in the leather.

"This document is very rare, indeed. It is a new acquisition and will be featured in our next auction. It has already generated quite a lot of interest."

Jennifer could almost see dollar signs reflected in the lenses of his eyeglasses.

The man slowly opened the case, revealing an old letter, the paper creased and brown with age. Tabitha reached to touch it.

"Ah, ah, ah! No touching! The oil from your skin can cause untold damage."

He handed Tabitha a magnifying glass and turned the document to face them, but Jennifer already recognized the letter as the same document her mother owned.

"Where did you come across such a find?" Jennifer asked innocently.

"The owner, Mr. Crotch, recently acquired it," the man said.

"Can you make a copy for us?" she asked him.

"Oh, dear me, no. The light from a copy machine would cause a level of deterioration. I can't allow it. I'm sorry."

Tabitha held up her cell phone. "Can I take a picture with my cell?"

"I will allow that, but no flash."

Tabitha took several shots. "Thanks, Mister!" she said, smiling. "This will get me a guaranteed A in class!" She turned to her mother. "Ready to go, Mom?"

At home, Jennifer had cleaned up the remains of their uneaten breakfast and started making dinner when the doorbell rang.

Tabitha jumped up and ran to the door. She looked though the peephole then shouted, "It's Dad!" She unlocked the door and threw herself into his arms.

Pete carried her inside, laughing.

Jennifer's phone rang. "Hello?" she said while she watched Tabitha pull Pete to the computer.

"Jennifer?" a man's voice asked.

"Yes," she answered, trying to place the caller. "Who is this?"

"Abner Crotch speaking."

"Oh," she said, taken by surprise. "Is everything okay with Mom?"

"Certainly. She's at home safe and sound after a rousing afternoon at bingo."

"Then what can I do for you?"

"My assistant mentioned you were at the shop earlier."

Jennifer felt her heart thump against her chest. How could he know that? She wasn't ready to confront him with the fact that he had stolen her mother's letter. She needed time to think, to strategize. Damn the man for catching her off guard!

"Um, oh, yes. Tabitha needed something for a school project. Something unusual. We stopped in several shops. Which one is yours?"

Abner laughed softly, the sound sending a shiver of fear deep into her soul. Pete and Tabitha, their attention focused on the computer, were oblivious to her distress.

"Jennifer. I know what you're thinking. But I can explain everything. I'm at the shop at present. Can you come over?"

"Now?"

"Yes. And I insist you come unaccompanied. This is a personal matter that does not require an audience."

"All right. I'm on my way," Jennifer said, ignoring the feeling of dread coursing through her body.

He laughed again.

"Excellent. The shop is closed, but I'll leave the front door unlocked for you."

Jennifer put the phone down and finished preparing dinner as if in a trance.

"Pete," she said.

"Yeah," he answered, turning from the computer. "I have the check." He got up and put a check on the kitchen counter.

"Thanks. Can you stay with Tabitha? I need to work tonight."

"Oh? Do you have a new client?"

"You could say that. Listen, there's lasagna in the oven. Just take it out when the timer goes off. I should be back in an hour at the most. Okay?"

Pete looked at Jennifer.

"Everything okay?"

Jennifer wanted to tell him about Abner, but stopped herself. He would interfere and tell her not to go. She picked up her purse and got out the car keys.

"Thanks, Pete."

The street in front of the Royal Antiques & Auction House was deserted when Jennifer pulled up at the curb. She wondered where Abner's car was. The neon sign had been turned off and the only light she could see came from the back of the shop. Across the street, Capital Park was dark and full of shadows. She got out of her car and shivered in the cold night air. An owl hooted. She walked to the shop and reached for the brass doorknob, but hesitated. Steeling her resolve, she pushed the door open, hearing the familiar tinkle of the bell.

"Jennifer?" Abner called out. "Is that you?"

"Yes. Where are you?"

"I'm in the back."

Jennifer stepped further into the store, but as she did she sensed something move beside her in the dark. Suddenly she felt a sharp blow at her head. Her world fragmented into a kaleidoscope of pain, and then she felt nothing as consciousness slipped away.

"Did Mom answer?" Tabitha asked her dad.

"No," Pete said, frowning. Two hours had passed and Jennifer should have been home by then. He took one last bite of lasagna and pushed his plate away.

"Maybe she's with Max," Tabitha suggested. She stood up to take their plates to the sink.

"I doubt it. From what I understood, your mom hadn't been able to get hold of him. I think he's hiding from the law."

Tabitha sat back down at the table.

"Dad? Are you going to arrest Max?"

He reached over and ran his hand along her cheek. "If there's enough evidence, I'll have to. It's my job, Tabby Cat. You know that."

Pete punched in Gramma's number.

"Rosie? It's Pete. Good. Good. But I'm here with Tabitha and we need to talk to Jennifer. Is she with you? No? No. Nothing's wrong. If you hear from her, have her give us a call. Okay? Thanks." He looked at his daughter.

"This isn't good," Tabitha said.

Pete stood up. "Let's go for a ride."

Max drove into the night, beside himself with grief. He was on autopilot, barely aware of his surroundings, his every move coming from some deep primal cortex in his brain. In one hand he clutched a golden wad of fabric. He rhythmically squeezed it, the effort focusing his brain on the task at hand as he headed to the Royal Antiques & Auction House.

Max saw Jennifer's car and parked behind it. What was she doing here? He looked across the street at the park where Sam had been found under a tree, strangled with a scarf or some kind of soft fabric, Pete had told him. He squeezed the golden ascot he'd found earlier in Sam's dresser drawer. The pattern of crowns on the fabric matched the crown on the awning of the antique shop. A keepsake, Max surmised, from his affair with that English dandy who was dating Jennifer's mother. Concern for Jennifer washed over him.

He walked to the front door of the auction house and tried the handle. Not surprisingly, the door was locked. Undeterred, he went around the building to the alley where he found Abner's car parked by a back door that led to the basement. Max went back to his car and opened the trunk, then he returned to the alley and stood in front of the door. In one hand, he squeezed the ascot, in the other, his clenched fist gripped a tire iron.

He needed to create a diversion to lure Abner out of the shop. He contemplated bashing in Abner's windshield and sounding the car alarm, but as he raised the tire iron, he heard the creak of the back door opening. Max quickly moved behind the door and held his breath. Abner poked his head out and looked down, his attention focused on propping the door open. Taking advantage of the situation, Max dropped the ascot and swung the tire iron with all his might. He heard a sickening crunch as the weapon connected with Abner's skull. Max jumped over the prone figure and rushed inside.

"Jennifer!" he shouted. "It's me, Max. Where are you?"

A muffled cry came from within the dark basement, the only source of light a bare bulb at the top of the stairs. Max searched the room and found Jennifer tied securely with duct tape to a dolly. He pulled the tape from her mouth and she gulped fresh air. Max ripped through the bindings, working down to her feet. When he stood up, Jennifer screamed at the gruesome sight of Abner, his face dripping blood, standing behind Max with the ascot stretched tight between his hands. Before Max could react, Abner wrapped the ascot against his neck and lifted him off his feet. As they struggled, Jennifer sprinted up the stairs, ignoring her pounding head, and into the shop where the Spanish sword lay on the counter as if waiting for her.

When consciousness returned, Max opened his eyes and stared at Jennifer, then he frantically scanned the room for Abner.

Jennifer lifted the Spanish sword and pointed upward. The light from the bare bulb reflected off the steel shaft, its tip now red with blood. "Argh. I took care of the land-lubber. He can't hurt anyone now."

The dolly leaned against a wall near the staircase, opposite from where Max and Jennifer sat. Abner was lashed firmly to it with yards of duct tape, his golden ascot used as a gag. Blood seeped from a large gash on his cheek and his eyes stared at them with naked hatred.

"Remind me never to challenge you to a sword fight," said Max.

Just then they heard sirens and the sound of glass shattering as police forced their way into the shop. The floorboards creaked above them and the basement door burst open. A strong flashlight beam swept down the stairs and around the room.

"Police! What is your situation?"

Jennifer recognized Pete's voice.

"You're clear, officer!" she shouted. "Suspect has been detained."

Abner produced a muffled cry from behind the ascot.

"You can come down now," she added.

Tabitha raced down the steps to her mother's side.

"Mom!" she said, hugging her tightly. "Are you okay?"

Jennifer smiled. "I might have a mild concussion, but I can handle a hug."

Jennifer told Pete everything she had learned from Abner before stuffing the golden ascot firmly into his mouth. "He confessed to the murder and to stealing Mom's letter while I held him at knife-point. Er, sword-point."

"Let me get this straight," Pete said, looking at Max. "He killed Sam out of jealousy because Sam refused to leave you?"

"That's right," said Max. "He used his own ascot to strangle him, then tied it back around his neck."

Jennifer broke in. "I told him there was enough DNA on it to prove he was the killer. And I'm sure you'll find the tires on the dolly match the tread pattern you found at the crime scene."

"See, Mom," said Tabitha, squeezing her tighter. "I told you we'd figure it out."

KAREN A. PHILLIPS works in Sacramento and lives in the Sierra foothills, often referred to as "Gold Country." She attributes her love of reading and writing to her mother whose eclectic book collection included *Portnoy's Complaint* and *Grimm's Fairy Tales*. Karen secretly dreams of one day becoming a best-selling author. But should this not come to fruition, her back-up plan is a Twiggy doll from her childhood that she hopes will one day be worth a small fortune.

DELTA SUICIDE
J. A. PIEPER

Josie Tawatao received the call from dispatch while jostling for the last of the season's zucchini at the Davis Farmers' Market. A death had been reported in the Sacramento-San Joaquin Delta. She looked into her reusable shopping bag at what was intended as the ingredients for a dinner party and sighed. But as she turned to weave her way out of the market to her bicycle, her adrenaline began pumping. She loved her work as assistant coroner for Yolo County, and she often boasted that she was never bored on the job.

While she was biking home, Detective Sergeant Marc Alvarez called to coordinate a meeting at the Rio Vista dock to launch the Yolo County Sheriff's boat and reach the crime scene together. They didn't always work together—Josie could be assigned to any sheriff team investigating a homicide—but she liked Marc. Marc said it was a possible suicide in the upper part of flooded Liberty Island. A suicide might not take all weekend to wrap up, but tonight's dinner party was definitely off. She sent a few texts while at stoplights to cancel her plans. By the time she reached home, she had focused on the job ahead.

She hurriedly put the entire unpacked shopping bag in the fridge and slipped from her yoga pants and elevated flip-flops into her jeans and wedge Sketchers. As someone who could pass for a Filipino kid, Josie catered to her one vanity, high heels, at all times. She pulled her jet black hair into a ponytail, threw on a grey hoodie and her Yolo County Coroner's windbreaker, and grabbed her bag of work gear and BMW car keys as she headed out the door.

As she sped past the Milk Farm on I-80, she called a colleague at the

Solano County Coroner's office to give a courtesy heads-up that she was crossing county lines to reach a body, a young woman in a kayak with a gunshot wound.

Josie was accustomed to responding to calls in the Delta. Bodies tended to surface after a big flood event, typically the largely decomposed remains of bridge jumpers and car accidents. Often they showed up in Elk Slough where Josie suspected the Sacramento County sheriff's deputies shifted them to get them out of their county and themselves out of the paperwork.

The 1,100 square mile Delta at the confluence of the Sacramento and San Joaquin rivers was a maze of islands channeled by armored levees. Nature and man continually competed for control in a confusing landscape bisected by five county boundaries. A GPS was standard operating equipment.

Marc guided the aluminum boat at top speed toward the waterway referred to as the Stairsteps because the unusually straight lines of an old irrigation canal looked like stair steps on an aerial map. The banks of the Stairsteps were overgrown with willows and tall grass on one side and tules on the other. Marc cut the engine to a putt-putt and this cued Josie to begin taking photos of the banks on either side.

The boat spooked a great blue heron roosting in a tree skeleton. Josie was startled but managed to snap a few frames as it slowly rose overhead and disappeared behind the tree line. Like Native Americans, she and Marc believed this bird to be an omen of a successful hunt. Whenever they worked in the Delta, they hoped to see one. Josie turned and caught Marc's smile in a camera click. Marc was remarkable for his personal energy, not his looks, and Josie hoped to one day capture his personality in a photo.

They were close to the crime scene and after another 90-degree turn of the canal, they saw the bass-fishing boat and the fisherman who had called in his gruesome find. Marc consulted his GPS one last time and steered around the bass boat, cutting the engine to drift until a kayak came into view. Josie already had their paddles out to guide them alongside the woman who lay awkwardly backward in the small boat.

This stretch of shoreline was a cattle pasture that dropped steeply into the water. The fisherman had wedged the kayak between his boat and the shoreline to keep it from drifting. A gunshot had sprayed blood, chest flesh and bits of clothing across the victim's beautiful face and the bright yellow plastic kayak. Josie thought something about the angle of the blast was off.

She donned gloves and reached into the kayak beside the victim and brought out a plastic bag containing UC Davis identification and car keys and handed it to Marc.

Marc pulled out his phone and called his deputy, Kevin Humphrey, back at the Woodland office. "Kev, I need you to find what you can about Rebekah Levin, R-E-B-E-K-A-H L-E-V-I-N." He paused and scanned the I.D. "She was a staff person in the UCD Entomology Department."

After a few moments, Kevin replied. "There's a record of calls to 911 for erratic behavior and possible suicide attempts. Looks like she's mental." Then Kevin's phone beeped. "This is dispatch. Let me get it and call you back."

Marc pocketed his phone and told Josie what Kevin had said, a possible suicide. "There's no gun, but it could have fallen into the water. We'll have to search for it."

"But the angle of the shot is wrong and what is this burn on the back of her neck?" Josie quietly observed. "Looks like from a strap or necklace that was pulled hard, maybe torn off."

"Yeah. From the pattern of the damage, I'd say this wasn't a suicide," Marc agreed.

Kevin called back. "Dispatch says her boyfriend called at 12:30 from the Bridge to Nowhere. They were supposed to meet there at 9:30, and when she didn't show, he called for help to search for her. Dispatch made the connection with this body."

"Okay. Send a deputy to the bridge to wait with him. We're closest so we'll interview him after the scene-of-the-crime team gets here. Is there a next of kin?"

"A sister in Sacramento."

"Go see her. Let her know that Rebekah has been fatally shot and ask her about her sister's state of mind as well as any possible threats."

Marc turned to the fisherman who had watched them glumly, hands shoved in his jeans pockets. The fisherman spat into the water then moved to the back of his boat and sat down, even though that made it harder for either Josie or Marc to see him.

"Permission to board?" Marc asked.

"Sure, yeah." He didn't look pleased, but Josie thought maybe shock was settling. His hands and shoulders shook. Marc grabbed a camouflage-hunting jacket from the back of the driver's seat and handed it to him, then took a small notebook and pen from his own pocket.

"May I have your name and occupation?"

"Jim Pierson. I work for Fish and Game. Not today. Today I'm fishing on my own time." Jim zipped up the jacket over his long-sleeved plaid cotton shirt with cowboy snaps. Instead of cowboy boots, he had muddy waterproof work boots. Jim's weathered face and hands made him look mid-thirties, but his sparse moustache suggested an age closer to late twenties.

"Did you catch anything?" Marc inquired.

"Yeah, a couple of stripers." Jim was sitting on the hatch of the well where bass fisherman kept their fish alive while still on the water.

"Did you hear anything?"

"Heard a lot of distant gunshots from the duck clubs." Jim rubbed one hand hard into the other palm. "I put my boat in at Freeport at sunrise, and I've been fishin' in the sloughs where there're no clubs. Don't like the feeling I might get shot. I was gonna take the Stairsteps down to the Bridge to Nowhere and then turn back. Needed to get home by noon for my son's soccer game. Once I found the body, I knew I couldn't just call it in and keep goin'."

"I'm missing my son's game, too," Marc said, "so I appreciate you doin' your civic duty. We'll need your home address and your work address and phone numbers."

Later that afternoon the team gathered around a picnic table at Husick's Deli in Clarksburg. Marc leaned forward, one tense hand gripping his Styrofoam cup of hot black coffee. "I interviewed the boyfriend. He's sure that Rebekah didn't commit suicide. She hated guns and used pills in her previous attempts."

Kevin took a sip of his hot chocolate with whipped cream. He was a small, powerful man with squinty eyes and a harelip. The contrast between his choice of drink and his dangerous demeanor always struck Josie as funny, but on this occasion she stuffed her joke away. Kevin could be a pain in the ass. She tried not to let him see she didn't like him.

Kevin added, "The sister agrees. No way it was a suicide. Rebekah was crazy—"

Josie interrupted, "Bipolar."

"Whatever. She'd been living on her meds for about 18 months and had a good job. The sister is begging us to investigate this as murder."

Josie took a swig of her root beer and swallowed. "What do you think of the boyfriend? He had opportunity and in any relationship there is always a motive."

"Isn't that a little cynical, Jo?" asked Kevin.

"I'm talking about passion, something you only have for killing helpless animals like deer and ducks."

"Back to our case," Marc said with a trace of irritation. "Who's out in the Delta on a Saturday morning?"

"Duck hunters. It's duck season," Kevin offered.

"Fisherman like our friend Jim," Josie quipped.

"Did you notice his weird energy?" Marc asked. "He acted guilty. We have to be careful not to read too much into it. Maybe he fished over the limit."

"Well, unless we can find a connection between Rebekah and Jim, we might be hard-pressed to find a motive," Josie said, staring at her root beer and peeling the label. "I was puzzled by the marks on her neck until her boyfriend told you she was an avid birder. So I asked him if Rebekah had binoculars. Apparently he'd given them to her for her birthday and she had them with her this morning."

"So you think the killer wrenched them off?" Kevin said doubtfully.

Marc watched Josie's fidgeting with the label. "What else?"

Josie sighed, "She was out in the middle of nowhere. Who else had the opportunity?"

"Right, who else is out there?" Marc asked. "Farmers, Fish and Game wardens—"

"On and off duty." Kevin added.

At that moment, Josie's phone vibrated. "It's Solano County. I left a message when I knew we'd have to cross the county line to pick up Rebekah's body." Josie mainly listened and when she hung up she looked grim.

"That was Samantha and she says they had a similar case two weeks ago. Someone in a canoe, and their team thought it a likely suicide."

Marc sprang to his feet, "Did they say who found the body?"

"No, I'll call back and get the details."

"I'll head back to the office to call Sacramento, Contra Costa and San Joaquin counties to see if they've had any similar cases." Marc crushed his coffee cup.

"You think it's a serial killer?" Kevin asked, more as confirmation of what they were all thinking.

Josie tore off the rest of the root beer label. "God help us," she said in a low, desperate whisper.

The team reconvened at the Woodland office on Monday morning at 7:00 a.m. sharp, each armed with a *venti* cup from Starbucks. Even though they'd logged long days on Saturday and Sunday gathering information and following up leads, they looked alert and anxious to get back in the field.

Marc's intense gaze at his notebook was the only clue to his anxiety about the case. In a steady voice, he summarized what he'd learned over the weekend from his colleagues in the other Delta counties.

"San Joaquin's victim was a lone fisherman shot in chest and ruled a suicide on opening day of duck season. Solano County had the canoeist in the Suisun Marsh with gunshot to the chest—that's the victim

Samantha told you about, Jo. The family persuaded the Solano sheriff to leave the case open, possible accident. In no case did the victims leave a suicide note."

"The first body was found by a duck hunter walking back from a blind and the second by another birder in a canoe, who knew the victim casually." Kevin read from his notes.

"Is there anything that connects these cases other than the general location?" Josie wondered aloud.

The three of them stared at a map on the wall marked with the crime scenes. The Delta, with its convoluted landscape of sloughs and channels, was hard to make sense of.

Marc tapped his pen. "He or she, though statistically it's more likely to be a male, has struck in a different county every time. Maybe that's a coincidence. There sure as hell aren't any county markers out there." They continued to stare at the map until Marc broke their concentration by swiveling to look at the white board with the victim's photos. "We've all read the victims' biographies," Marc observed. "There doesn't seem to be anything that links the three to each other or to a possible fourth person."

"There's Jim Pierson who lied about his kid playing soccer," Kevin said with some satisfaction. "I was able to reach his supervisor, and he told me Pierson's wife and son moved to Montana a couple of months ago. His attendance at work has been spotty ever since."

"But why would he stay with the body if he was the killer?" Josie asked. "And the angle of the shot was wrong unless he was on land."

Marc refocused. "Okay, before we get fixated on any one suspect, let's look at the pattern. Why Wednesdays and Saturdays?"

"As the outdoorsman on our team," Kevin said with an arrogant grin, "those are traditionally the busiest days during duck season. A rifle shooting on one of those mornings—if not ruled a suicide—might pass as accidental."

"And no one would think twice about hearing a gunshot because all of the murders took place near duck clubs." Josie added.

They stared harder at the map. Kevin broke the silence. "If it is a serial killer, how the hell do we figure out where he might strike next?"

"Alright, we are burning daylight." Marc took another hard look at the white board. "Kev, you work on finding a connection between any of the victims and Jim Pierson. If this killer follows the pattern, he may strike again this Wednesday. We'd better use the time we have strategically."

Josie remained seated staring at the map. She remembered a PhD student she'd met at a party in Davis who was building a hydrologic model of the Delta. What was her name? She knew the landscape intimately. Wendy. Maybe if she talked through the locations with Wendy, a pattern would emerge.

Tuesday morning the team met again, Marc and Kevin looking deflated. They had no breakthroughs to report. Josie, the exception; couldn't wait to share the results of her brainstorm with Wendy.

"Jim's life has definitely gone off the rails," Kevin began. "His family left him. Then a neighbor reported a domestic disturbance, but his girlfriend hightailed it before officers arrived. His coworkers say his finances are in shambles, and he is spending more and more time on the river."

"Is there any way to tell where he was for the first two murders?" Marc asked.

"Yeah," Kevin replied, "his supervisor says that his job is to collect data from a series of stations that run from Freeport to Suisun Marsh, and on the days of the other murders he was in the vicinity."

"I admit there is a lot of circumstantial evidence," Josie said impatiently. "But I just can't see a motive for staying with Rebekah's body, or returning to the scene to report it. We've got to consider that the Delta is a big place and there could be a killer who isn't on our radar yet, and who doesn't need to know his victim, just needs some hapless hunter or boater to go by the slough where he waits."

Marc shifted in his chair uncomfortably, "I know, Josie, but this is the proverbial needle in a haystack. We can't stage a dragnet over every slough and along every levee."

"I understand," Josie said in a torrent of words, "that's why I spent a couple of hours studying the map of the crime scenes with an expert on Delta geography. We think we've found a pattern involving public access and wooded areas with intermittent open spaces alongside steep banks. There are other indicators, too, but the important thing is that there isn't a location that fits in Contra Costa County, so the next strike will probably be in Sacramento County, or what the killer thinks is Sacramento County, probably somewhere along Elk Slough."

"Elk Slough is a long shot and we could easily miss him," Kevin argued. "But if we stake out Jim's apartment and follow him on Wednesday morning, we'll be able to determine whether he is a killer or just a loser on a downward spiral."

Marc looked pensive as he sat silently for several minutes during which Josie worked hard to suppress several urges to speak and endured Kevin's resentful glare.

"Josie, your idea is too risky," Marc said with finality. "I agree with Kevin that our best bet is to follow Jim on Wednesday morning. Kevin and I will arrange the stakeout and we'll keep you posted."

Josie gathered up her notes and left the room without looking at Kevin. She walked toward the coroner's offices as she texted her neighbor with a kayak. No risk, no reward, she thought as she went back to her office to print out the Google Earth files Wendy had given her.

The next day, Jim Pierson left for work at 5:30 a.m. so following him was relatively easy before dawn. Kevin and Marc were in the same vehicle. A deputy waited with a boat already in the water in Freeport if Jim showed up for work as expected, and another boat was standing by on a trailer in Clarksburg if Jim led them on a detour. Pierson followed his work routine, however, and soon Kevin, Marc and the other deputy were trailing him at a discreet distance on the Sacramento River. This became more challenging as the sun rose until Jim steered right at Elk Slough, and the natural bends in the slough allowed them to stay out of Jim's sight range.

Josie launched her kayak at Clarksburg and paddled toward the sea along Elk Slough wearing layers of quick-dry clothes made more uncomfortable by a bulletproof vest and life jacket. At least, the vests kept her warmer. The westerly breeze was bone chilling, and Josie clenched her teeth tightly to keep them from chattering. She had her camera around her neck and she concentrated on her stroke, trying to remember the most efficient rhythm. "I hope it's like riding a bike," she said aloud to the quiet water.

Occasionally, she set her paddle on her bow and took pictures of the hint of a sunrise and of the banks of the slough before picking up her paddle and continuing another hundred yards. She had done this several times when she saw something orange-red through the trees, like the warning color of a hunter's jacket. Josie felt a surge of electric energy up her spine and her senses became more acute.

The tide in the slough was counter-intuitive—you'd expect the current to pull from the valley to the sea, but the pull was softened or strengthened by the tide. The closer you got to the sea, the more the tidal action dominated. Here in the north Delta, the tide was coming in and only weakened the downstream current. This allowed Josie to move downstream toward the red jacket more slowly and gave her time to move to the far side of the slough.

As Josie floated past the suspicious fabric, she repeated her routine of taking pictures of the sunrise and the slough banks, but this time her heart was beating so hard she wondered if she'd keep her camera steady. Through the lens she saw a duck hunter slumped on the bank in a stretch that wasn't wooded, just as in all the other crime scenes.

He did not move while she floated by taking photos. Was this the killer's M.O.? Or was this a new victim or someone self-injured? She floated round a bend past the hunter and pulled her phone out of her pocket. Voices carried easily in the slough's quiet, so she quickly texted her location to a colleague and added, call for backup.

Josie turned her kayak and began paddling upstream towards the man on the bank, this time from the middle of the slough. "Hey, are you okay?" she shouted. The man did not move a muscle. "Are you hurt?"

Once past him, Josie found herself strangely compelled to turn her boat and float past much closer to his side of the shore. Just as she neared the duck hunter, she shifted her paddle to be able to poke him or protect herself. At almost the same moment, the duck hunter moved with amazing agility and lunged at her camera. Josie's paddle came crashing down on his outstretched hand, but she struggled to hang on to her paddle and keep her balance. A rush of icy river water swept over the kayak deck. Don't. Tip. Over. Josie thought. The hunter let go of the camera strap and fell backward on to the bank. Josie's kayak twisted and now she was facing upstream. In a burst of adrenaline-fueled paddling, she kicked her kayak forward.

She heard a crack that sounded like thunder and waited for impact. None. She didn't look back and paddled in a whole new gear. When she finally looked to the side, she glimpsed the duck hunter chasing her on foot above the tree line on top of the levee. Her anger and fear drove her to dig deeper into the water.

Faintly, she heard a boat motor from further upstream. Maybe someone else was nearby. She willed herself to paddle but could feel her arms tiring. The motor noise grew louder as she paddled to the far side of the slough. Then she saw a Fish and Game boat approaching. Josie wondered in her growing fatigue if she was hallucinating.

The duck hunter's red jacket slowed on the levee and began to retreat as Josie paddled alongside Jim Pierson's boat. He killed his motor and moved nearer. "Miss?" he said in recognition.

In that same moment, Marc and Kevin's boat sped toward them from around the bend upstream. The third deputy was just picking up the message from dispatch with the coordinates from Josie's call for back up. Kevin slowed the boat and glided alongside Josie and Jim.

"Josie?" Marc shouted angrily.

Josie could barely catch her breath to speak. "He's on... right bank. Red jacket." She looked at Jim's puzzled face as he hung over the side of his boat to hang on to her kayak. In the distance was the unmistakable sound of a police siren from the levee road.

Kevin gunned the sheriff's boat past them and in the direction Josie had pointed. He and Marc had their weapons ready. They were just out of sight when Josie and Jim heard a gunshot.

Josie slowly paddled downstream to the spot where the duck hunter had first feigned injury. Josie saw that this time it was no fake: self-inflicted gunshot wound to the chest. No question, this was a suicide.

J. A. PIEPER is a life-long mystery fan who recently redesigned her life to create more time to write. This short mystery is her publishing debut. She is editing her first mystery novel, set in New Zealand. A long-time resident of Sacramento, she recently moved to Davis with her old dog where she also enjoys cycling, gardening, knitting, and reading. Her day job takes her regularly into the Sacramento-San Joaquin Delta.

THE CASE OF THE CARAMELIZED CORPSE
CINDY SAMPLE

"Caramel apples are my favorite," Shelly said to her partner. "The thicker the caramel, the better."

"Yep, when I think of autumn, I think of food—apple cider, apple donuts and candy apples." Buck patted his khaki-clad belly. His shirt, which looked ready to burst a button or two, demonstrated his love of Apple Hill delights. Buck stepped back and snapped a few more photos. "And Halloween ghosts and goblins, of course."

Shelly stared at the body of Hans Alder, the now deceased owner of Happy Apple Farm, who lay in the dry streambed at the bottom of a grassy knoll. "I doubt if a ghost or goblin did this."

Buck shot one more picture of the corpse. The *caramel-coated corpse.* "Probably not. Whoever killed Hans was one angry dude."

"Or dudette." Shelly brushed aside some dried leaves from the body with gloved fingers. She pinched a long strand of blonde hair off the corpse and stuck it in an evidence bag. The hair was barely noticeable against the shiny, sticky and sickeningly sweet body of the victim. It didn't come from Shelly's dark braid, their bald victim or the creature that had discovered the body.

Was the killer trying to make a saccharine point?

Detective Tom Hunter walked up behind Shelly, echoing her thoughts. "Any chance this was an accident?"

Shelly narrowed her hazel eyes at her boss, the head of the homicide division for the El Dorado County Sheriff's Department. "Let's see. We have a guy covered from head to toe in hot caramel whose body was dumped outside."

All three officers stared at the dead man. "Nah," they said in unison.

"Whoever it was sure had a grudge against him," muttered Detective Hunter. "I wonder how long he'd have been hidden if that bear hadn't been looking for breakfast."

Shelly eyed the long streaks on the body where the bear had licked caramel off. "Good thing he didn't gnaw off any evidence."

"Yeah, I hate searching for body parts." Hunter shoved his hands in the pockets of his leather bomber jacket. "How did he end up in the creek bed?"

"The kitchen up there is where they make the apples." Shelly pointed to a yellow building at the top of the hill. "I suppose he could have been 'glazed' then shoved down the hill."

"Any suspects?" Hunter asked.

"A few. All his co-workers on the morning shift. Two busloads of school kids, a group of Red Hat ladies and several hundred visitors," Buck said. "The reason we were originally called was that the black bear appeared and scared the dickens out of the tourists. When Randy arrived to track the bear's whereabouts, he discovered the body."

Randy, a new deputy with the Sheriff's Department, slumped on a wooden bench thirty yards away. His face matched the color of the lawn surrounding the picnic area. Shelly could commiserate. Despite her ten years with the department, she was starting to feel nauseous herself. This murder was going to put her off carbs for a good twenty-four hours.

Evidently Buck didn't face the same dilemma. His stomach roared louder than the tractor driving down the road. He threw Shelly a sheepish grin. "Sorry, I skipped breakfast. Can you get me one of those apple dumplings when you go back to the apple barn?"

Shelly rolled her eyes at him then climbed up the hill to meet the lab guys. Dark storm clouds covered the sky. She shivered, feeling the chill in the air through her uniform shirt. Two days ago it had been eighty degrees and bright blue skies. Today the sky looked ready to dump a foot of snow all over the crime scene.

A cold day. And a cold-blooded murder.

The crime scene techs arrived and she ushered them to the body. "You better hurry up, guys, he's starting to harden."

The younger of the two looked confused. "You mean the caramel coating?"

When would they stop hiring recruits right out of school? "No. Rigor mortis. Do your job so we can get him out of here."

His partner sniggered, "Well, at least, he doesn't have a stick shoved up his..."

Rookies!

It was time for her to interview witnesses and potential suspects. Shelly could probably rule out the busloads of children, although kids were exposed to so much television violence these days, they might see caramel coating as a terrific prank.

It was highly unlikely the Red Hat ladies were guilty of anything more severe than a crime of fashion. She winced as her gaze landed on one woman dressed in a sequined purple tee shirt and matching capris. A red straw hat larger than Shelly's turkey platter perched on her short silver hair. A few aisles over, a tall woman dressed in a puffy purple parka and red hat replete with veil, perused the specialty jams and jellies.

Talk about scary!

Her first thought was to determine whether anyone wore clothes marred with sticky caramel. After strolling through the rustic apple barn, Shelly decided almost every visitor's face, hands and apparel bore traces of caramel.

Yellow crime scene tape barricaded the employees from the bakery. The kitchen staff sat around a rectangular wooden table in the rear of the main dining room. All wore matching black polo shirts with the Happy Apple logo, a large red apple engraved with a smiley face. Despite the cheery logo, there was nary a smiley face to be found among the five women seated at the table. Their conversation quieted as she approached.

"Hello, ladies," she said. "I'll be interviewing each of you individually. Is there a private area where we can meet?"

One woman spoke up. "We can use Hans' office. Or the cider barn?"

"The office is sealed off. The cider barn it is."

Shelly spent the next hour interviewing the staff. The women all looked terrified, but she couldn't tell if they were worried about losing their jobs or losing their boss. None of the ladies shed a single tear during the interview. They only wanted to know when they could go back to work.

Darlene Taylor, a mature woman who wore sensible shoes and her long gray hair in a sensible bun, ran the kitchen. She'd worked at the farm for five years but had only been promoted to manager two months earlier. Shelly saved her questioning for last.

Darlene gave Shelly a tour of the back room where the staff coated and decorated the apples. Enormous kettles of hot golden caramel simmered over large propane burners. Huge plastic bins containing rainbow-covered sprinkles, chocolate and toffee chips and assorted nuts lined the shelves. The staff had been fingerprinted and the kitchen area dusted and investigated by the crime scene guys, but Shelly wanted to get a better feel for the operation.

"Who has access to this area besides the staff?" Shelly asked.

Darlene pointed to the door in the back. "That's open all day but locked at night."

"Was it locked when you arrived this morning?"

Darlene face grew paler than the container of powdered sugar next to her. "No, but that wasn't unusual. Hans was normally the first to arrive. He would check his emails then make the rounds of the cider barn and shops. Hans loved inventing new candy apple combinations, so it wasn't unusual for him to fire up the burners and heat up a fresh batch of caramel before the staff arrived."

"Can you think of anyone who'd want to kill him?"

Darlene hesitated before she nodded. A half hour later, Shelly realized it wasn't a question of *who* wanted Hans Alder dead. Finding someone who *didn't* want him dead was more of an issue.

Happy Apple Farm's location at 3,000 feet elevation in the Apple Hill area of Camino, approximately fifty miles east of Sacramento, provided the perfect conditions for growing apples, pears and a variety of grapes. In the early 1960s, Hans's father had turned the family orchard into a pie-making business. Eventually tourists from Sacramento and the Bay Area discovered the autumnal beauty of Apple Hill.

After his father died, Hans expanded the farm into the largest commercial enterprise in the area. His staff baked pies, cakes, cobblers, and donuts. They produced every type of caramel, cinnamon, or chocolate-covered apple one could desire. A variety of gift shops and a winery were added a few years later.

Rumors abounded about the victim's cutthroat nature. When two of the farms next to Happy Apple couldn't make the payments on their mortgages, he offered to help them out by buying the paper from the bank. Then he promptly foreclosed on his neighbors, adding to his land holdings.

A winery across the street that produced award-winning wines accused Hans of sabotaging their crop of zinfandel grapes in September.

Hans fired Darlene's predecessor in August.

He was in the middle of a hotly contested divorce.

Shelly was up to her need-to-be-tweezed eyebrows in suspects. But was the murder premeditated or a spontaneous act of passion? Motive was one thing. Opportunity another.

Unfortunately, based on Darlene's comments, anyone could have entered the building. The staff was familiar with Han's morning routine. The victim was only five foot five, so it would not have been difficult to drag him out the door and shove him down the hill. As the body picked up momentum, leaves had affixed themselves to the sticky substance. By the time Hans landed in the dry creek bed, he'd become camouflaged from sight.

But not from smell. Smokey the Bear had no problem following his sickeningly sweet scent.

Buck joined her in the picnic area as she examined her notes. Marshmallow flecks dotted his sandy moustache as he shared a sticky smile.

"What have you discovered?" Shelly asked.

"They got the best caramellows here." He licked his fingers. "That dumpling was mighty fine, too."

Sigh. She could tell it would be a long day.

"Did you interview the guys in the cider barn?"

Buck pulled out a steno pad from his shirt pocket. "Yep, they got a staff of five guys who work different shifts, two to three men during the week, more on the weekends if necessary. You should see this old timey machine they got." Buck snapped his fingers. "It peels, cores and slices the apples just like that."

"Any of them have a motive to kill him? Did they alibi out?"

"The three guys working today were in and out all morning. If they're caught up with slicing apples for the pies and making cider, they sometimes help in other areas. This place is a regular beehive of activity in late October."

"Great," she sighed. "They all had opportunity."

He shrugged. "Yeah, but no motive as far as I can tell. It's kind of weird though. It's not like folks is jumping up and down for joy, but I sure didn't get the impression the employees were going to miss old Hans."

It was beginning to look like Happy Apple Farm wasn't the happiest place in town.

"Did anyone notice anything suspicious earlier this morning? Any cars or trucks that didn't belong to staff members?" Shelly could feel the anxiety that accompanied each new case file, ooze into her pores. Far too many people had tromped all over the crime scene.

Some days she wished she still styled hair for a living. Screwing up someone's haircut might result in the loss of a client. Screwing up a murder investigation meant a killer remained on the loose.

That reminded her of the blonde strand of hair she had picked off the victim and dropped off with the crime scene guys. Hunter might want the DNA checked, although the state was so far behind in DNA testing, it could be Easter before they got the results.

Randy joined Shelly and Buck. "Can we let these folks go home? I took everyone's name, address and phone number. The little kids are getting antsy. And those Red Hat ladies. Geez. That old bat—" He stopped as Shelly eyeballed him. "I mean lady in charge—said this delay has put them off their schedule."

"Yeah, murder can do that," Shelly replied. She wondered if the women were members of a local group. Her mother went on outings such as this with her own Red Hat club each month. Shelly had dubbed them the Mad Hatters. She still couldn't figure out why turning fifty made it okay for women to dress and act outrageously. Maybe it was a hormonal thing. Her mother claimed living in an estrogen-free zone made for non-stop happiness.

Of course, Mom didn't chase killers for a living.

Hunter walked up to confer with them. "They're taking the body to the morgue. Where are we at?"

Shelly led them over to a picnic table so they could update their boss. The sun peeked from behind the clouds, burnishing the red and golden leaves of the maples and Chinese pistache trees. She hoped the sun's rays were a positive sign because so far this case was getting colder by the minute.

Hunter eased his six-foot-three frame on to the bench on one side of the wooden table. Shelly and Buck sat across from him. Randy left to deal with the release of the farm visitors.

"From the information Buck and I gathered from the staff," Shelly said, "no one saw anything suspicious by a fellow employee or an outsider. Hans isn't the most popular guy in town, however. He foreclosed on his former neighbors a couple of months ago, so they definitely had a grudge. There's also a rumor going around that Hans sabotaged Belleville Vineyards, but they had no proof, so no lawsuit was filed."

Buck jumped in. "He fired the previous manager two months ago. Supposedly she threatened Hans. Maybe she caramelized her old boss."

"You've got your work cut out for you," Hunter said. "You need to interview them today if possible."

Swell. Shelly looked at her boss. "What should I do with the Happy Apple staff? Tell them to go home?"

Hunter drummed his fingers on the table. "Who owns the farm in the event of Hans's death? You didn't mentioned any heirs. This place must be worth a good chunk of change."

"I'm not completely clear on that. Darlene thought Hans's about-to-be ex was still half owner, which is the reason their divorce has dragged on so long. They couldn't come to a financial agreement."

Hunter frowned. "Why didn't you include her as a suspect?"

"She's been in Seattle the last two days. I already verified she is flying home tonight. Hard to kill someone long distance."

Her boss snorted. "Given the way technology is changing, pretty soon you'll be able to hire a virtual assassin straight from Amazon."

Buck hooted. "I'm glad I'll be retired by then. Nothing beats old-fashioned legwork. Which reminds me, I should stock up on some old-fashioned snacks before we take off to interview them other suspects." He unfurled his long legs and loped up the hill toward the bakery.

Shelly threw her arms up in frustration and her notepad flew into the air. Her boss laughed, handed the pad back to her and told her to get a move on. She watched Tom Hunter as he strode off, cell phone glued to his ear. He was tall, with a great build and a natural grace of movement. She wondered if there was any truth to the rumor he was dating that soccer mom who was involved in a murder investigation a while back.

Good men were hard to find. And even harder to keep. Once she disclosed that she worked homicide, Shelly rarely got asked out on a second date. At this rate, she'd never have a hot date again.

The only men in her life would be cold and stiff. And residents of the morgue.

Shelly reviewed her notes to make sure she didn't forget anything while she was still at the scene. Her tenacity and attention to detail were one of the reasons the sheriff had promoted her. At thirty-two, she was the youngest detective on the force.

Car engines rumbled as families began driving away. Most folks were leaving empty- handed, although a few held white paper bags filled with goodies they'd purchased earlier. The visitors ranged from tiny infants tucked into their snuggly carriers to elderly couples hobbling on canes and walkers. The Red Hatters stood out from the crowd like a flock of cardinals surrounded by an army of wrens. Two of the six women were climbing into the back seat of a large black SUV. One tried entering without removing her platter-sized hat. It bounced off her head, but she quickly retrieved the Frisbee-shaped object from the ground.

Eventually the women and their oversized hats made it into the large vehicle and they drove off. The minute they disappeared, Shelly realized she should have inquired where they purchased their hats. A new red hat would be the perfect gift for her mother's birthday tomorrow.

Shelly went back to reviewing Randy's notes about the visitors, their addresses and any observations. He'd categorized families and other small groups together. All six Red Hatters were listed with their names and phone numbers. She could always call them regarding their chapeaux.

Her partner joined her, an enormous paper bag clutched to his chest.

"Buck, where are you getting all this food?"

He shuffled his feet. "Darlene felt sorry for me and made me a goody bag. They had tons of stuff left over once we shut down the cash registers. She told me a little sugar never hurt no one."

Not exactly true. An excess of hot caramelized sugar had seared their victim to death. Shelly wondered if a carb infusion might energize her brain cells. Buck offered his bag and she peeked inside. One donut wouldn't kill her.

She bit into the apple-filled pastry. Yum. This apple farm really was a gold mine. Hans's ex-wife could luck out with Hans out of the picture. How often was an ex-spouse murdered before a contested divorce was finalized?

The donut dropped out of her hand and on to the ground as she puzzled over the question. How often *did* a murder benefit the spouse?

Frequently. But Dina Alder had a bullet-proof alibi. She was in Seattle when the killing occurred. Shelly mulled over Tom Hunter's comment about hiring a virtual assassin via the internet. Could the woman have paid someone to do her dirty work? What precipitated the divorce in the first place?

Shelly picked up the dirt-covered donut, dumped it in a garbage can then returned to the apple barn. Darlene already had her pea coat on and her purse slung over her shoulder. Shelly motioned for her to wait.

"Thanks so much for your help today, Darlene. I have one more question if you don't mind."

"Of course."

"Do you know why the Alders were getting a divorce?"

The manager pursed her lips. "I hate to spread rumors."

"Spread away. There is no such thing as a rumor when a murder needs to be solved."

"Okay. Dina Alder took up with a much younger guy. A musician. When Hans first accused her of having an affair, she claimed she was only trying to help him get discovered." Darlene folded her arms together. "I can just imagine that discovery process."

"What's his name? Can you describe him?"

"Not sure of his name. Michael something or other. It was kind of hi-falutin'. But he's tall, slender, with longish blond hair."

Shelly wrote quickly in her shorthand fashion. A hi-falutin' name wasn't particularly helpful, but his description could be. Who would know his name?

Shelly thanked Darlene then walked toward the parking lot. She and Buck had a long day and night ahead of them. Most of the visitors had dispersed by now. The few stragglers were probably getting a kick out of being involved in a murder investigation.

CSI comes to Happy Apple Farm.

Shelly noticed the tall woman she'd seen earlier walking toward the parking lot. The one dressed in the ugly purple parka and red veiled hat. Her mother would love that hat. Very Mata Hari.

Shelly headed toward the woman to inquire where she'd purchased her hat. Then her jaw dropped as she did a head count. There was a seventh member of the Red Hat group here today?

Shelly paused and grabbed her notebook, scrolling through the list of interviewees. Buck had listed six Red Hat ladies, not seven. Was this one a lone red hatter?

That would be odd. Mad Hatters always traveled in a pack. And they normally drove sedans and SUVs. Not white Toyota pick-ups with bumper stickers that said *Make it with a Musician*.

The woman backed out of her parking space then shifted into drive. Shelly's heart raced faster than the truck engine as she pumped her legs forward. She needed one last glimpse of the woman before she disappeared.

From thirty feet away, her eyes met the dark gaze of the driver. His long blond hair curled over the collar of his parka. Shelly reached for her gun then realized there were too many people in the vicinity. It would be crazy to attempt to shoot out his tire. She would never forgive herself if she accidentally hurt an innocent bystander.

Instead Shelly reached into her pocket and shot him with something else.

"Nice work, partner." Buck walked into the sheriff's office gnawing on a Golden Delicious apple surrounded by thick caramel. One of the many treats Darlene had packed for him.

Sometimes Shelly wished she were a foot taller so she could inhale food like Buck did and not gain a pound. Although after today's events, she could go the rest of her life without ever eating another caramel apple.

She smiled at Buck. "Not often we can solve a murder in less than twenty-four hours."

"Smart move using your phone to shoot a photo of the murderer's license plate."

"We're lucky he was one of those lurker killers," Shelly said. "He couldn't resist watching the aftermath of his crime."

"They came up with a clever concept. No one would suspect a Red Hat lady. Despite their crazy get-ups, they sort of blend into the surroundings. How did he know there would be a group there today?"

"Dina Alder knows one of the members. She's the one who suggested they visit today. Originally she told the group she would give them a special tour. Then she arranged the last- minute trip to Seattle as her alibi."

"Not a bad plan. They might have gotten away with it if it wasn't for you."

"Thanks. I'm going to print out my report and head home. It's my mother's birthday tomorrow and we're going to spend the day together."

"Have fun." Buck strolled out the door crunching on his apple.

Shelly's cell rang and she grabbed it. "Hi, Mom. Looking forward to your birthday tomorrow?"

"Of course, dear. And I know where I want to go to celebrate."

"It's your special day. Whatever you want."

Shelly pictured her mother's warm smile as the older woman's voice bubbled over the phone. "I can't think of a happier place than Happy Apple Farm, can you?"

CINDY SAMPLE is a former mortgage banking CEO who retired to follow her lifelong dream of becoming a mystery author. Her humorous romantic mystery series set in El Dorado County features single soccer mom, Laurel McKay. Her first book, *Dying for a Date*, was released in 2010. The sequel, *Dying for a Dance*, was a finalist for the 2012 LEFTY award for best humorous mystery and recipient of the 2012 NCPA award for Best Fiction. Cindy is a past president of Capitol Crimes. She is currently working on *Dying for a Daiquiri* and loving the research. Visit Cindy at www.CindySampleBooks.com.

DEATH VALLEY REDUX
LINDA TOWNSDIN

A trip to Death Valley on the spur of the moment was so typical of Victor. Eyes bright, he coaxed, "A guy at the gym said it's a great place to hike."

His enthusiasm for adventure was what had attracted Ashley to him in the first place, but she couldn't begin to match her husband's strength and endurance, despite being fifteen years younger than his forty-seven. Not that he expected her to do everything he did, but he expected her to be there.

"I'm not feeling well." She sat in her chintz chair beside the fireplace and hugged her stomach.

He stood over her. "Ash, it won't be the same if you don't come with me. We always take our vacations together."

He must have forgotten how she suffered in the sun. "Remember Brazil?" she asked.

She'd gotten the worst burn of her life on a beach in Puerto Allegra when they were newly married. Her skin had peeled off in sheets and she'd spent their first vacation together in the hospital.

He showed her photos on the Death Valley tourist information website, "The hotel has a huge pool. You can stay cool while I hike."

"But June is my favorite month in Sacramento. Everything's blooming."

"It's only a weekend." He dropped into his black leather recliner across from her and glared.

If she didn't go, he wouldn't. He'd sulk. How bad could it be? Besides, this hiking trip might put him in a good mood. She needed to tell him her secret.

"C'mon," he said. "We've never been to the desert. Don't be a wimp."

They never vacationed in the same place twice, no matter how much they enjoyed it. "Too much to see and do," he said. "There's no point in doing the same things over and over."

He decided where they would go; she handled the details. When she protested they didn't have the money to go to Europe eight years ago, and they should use their tax refund to pay off the large credit card bill, he'd said, "It's not like we have to save for college educations like my brother. With four kids, they can't do anything anymore."

One year they went to Jamaica and stayed at an inn run by a woman artist. Ashley took a watercolor lesson while Victor went deep-sea fishing. When he returned, he talked about the big marlin he'd caught and she showed him her sketch of a group of children playing tag in the white sand. A little girl had made a sand castle next to Ashley, and Ashley had gotten lost in the child's aquamarine eyes. With strawberry-red hair and freckles, she could have been Ashley's own daughter.

Victor had jabbed a finger at her sketch. "While we're relaxing over a bottle of Cabernet at that restaurant with the waterfall, those parents will be treating sunburns and trying to get overexcited kids ready for bed." He held her close and whispered in her ear. "We're lucky we love each other so much. We don't need anyone else."

Ashley's artwork now covered the walls of their Sacramento home: framed watercolors and oil paintings of children playing in the sand on Oahu or skiing down the bunny trail in Aspen covered head to toe in snow, cheeks and noses bright pink. One of Ashley's favorites was the five-year-old with long golden braids tied with mismatched ribbons. Standing on the bridge at Monet's historic home in Giverny, she'd pointed at the water lilies and said, "Look, mama, just like in the painting!"

Victor said they had the ideal life, and yet Ashley often looked at her wall of children and pretended they were her own. She imagined them together in all those places, instead of drawn from a distance.

Victor didn't think it practical to have a family because their careers involved lots of travel. Whenever they took off on vacation, he'd say, "We certainly couldn't be doing this right now if we had kids. We'd be paying for orthodontia." He might substitute some other expense like private school or tutoring.

And now she was pregnant and didn't know how to tell him she wanted her baby. Until this accident happened, she hadn't known how strongly she felt about it. She knew he'd talk her into an abortion. He'd talk and talk until she wouldn't remember why she wanted a child.

They arrived at the Death Valley hotel mid-day on Friday after driving through miles of sand dunes. They passed rock formations with undulating ripples of green, lavender and rose pink shot through with slashes of black and pure white. She had not expected that riot of color. Her brochure said the colors came from different minerals, but she didn't really care how it happened. She enjoyed the drama of light and shadow playing over a ridge and the illusion that you could walk forever. But nothing was as it seemed. Sand dunes that appeared to be a few hundred yards ahead were, in fact, miles away and tall as mountains.

They ate breakfast Saturday at the historic Furnace Creek Inn. Victor opened his map to show her a hike he wanted to take up a peak called Zabriskie Point, even though June was late in the season to hike. Because of the intense heat, most of the tourists were gone. The hotel manager told them that only the Europeans traveled through the Valley during the summer. "They like to experience the heat, but mostly from their air-conditioned rental cars. Usually they are not big hikers."

Ashley picked at her kiwi and strawberries and told her husband about an article she'd read in the National Park Service newsletter.

"A man from Sweden decided to hike Zabriskie Point. At the appointed time, his wife was waiting at a spot where they agreed to meet. Only he didn't show up." She paused for effect. "It was noon and well over 100 degrees. Finally, she got a park ranger to look for him, and they found him dead from heatstroke. When he came down from Zabriskie Point, he'd walked in the opposite direction."

Victor folded his map and flashed his wide white grin. "I'm not some guy from Scandinavia who doesn't know how to hike in hot weather. You know me better than that."

Victor left to tour a canyon with a group of people led by Ranger Mike. Ashley floated face down in the hotel pool's cool water, the midday sun warming her back. She had to be careful of developing an itchy skin rash. On their trip to Hawaii, she'd worn long-sleeved tops and large-brimmed hats until the sun poisoning subsided and she could enjoy being outside again. Only by then it was time to leave.

Someone poked her in the side. She put her head out of the water and looked into a pair of big brown eyes.

"You looked dead," said the boy.

Ashley smiled at him. "I was just playing dead. Not *really* dead. What's your name?"

"Jacob." He pointed to a woman reading on a bench under a canopy of trees. A short ponytail stuck out the back of her baseball cap. "That's my mom.

"Hey, Mom," he yelled. "The lady wasn't dead, see!"

The woman looked up from her book, "Don't bother her, Jacob. Play with your sister."

"It's fine, really," said Ashley.

Jacob told Ashley about the lizard he'd caught that morning. She thought that if she and Victor had a son he would have her husband's snapping brown eyes and thick, chestnut curls like Jacob's. Jacob even had the same assertive manner as her husband, a certain attitude of entitlement to her undivided attention. She could picture a daughter more easily. Her name would be Chloe.

When Jacob saw his sister getting ready to dive, he lost interest in Ashley. "Jump, jump!"

Jacob's sister cannonballed into the middle of the pool and the two of them chased each other in slow motion through the water, yelling and splashing. Ashley swam to the side and pulled herself up the ladder. A sharp pain caused her to double over. After a minute it subsided and she climbed out of the pool. She grabbed her bag and towel and sat on the bench beside the woman.

"Your children are delightful," she said.

"I'm guessing that's your polite way of saying wild." The woman grimaced, "They're a handful." She put her hand out. "My name's Jillian."

"I'm Ashley."

A toddler, digging in the playground sandbox, yelped and ran to Jillian. "My toe got burned." Jillian scooped her up, brushed the sand off her toe and kissed it, then tightened the buckle on her sandal and sent her back to play. "Stay in the shade, sweetie."

Ashley took out her sketchpad and colored pencils and sketched Jacob chasing his sister in the water.

Jillian asked, "You have kids?"

"Not yet, but we want to." Ashley wondered why she'd said that. "I'm an event planner in Sacramento and I'm constantly traveling to trade shows and conferences. My husband's a salesman for the same organization so we're always away." Ashley looked out at the desert, missing the canopies of trees at home, where she could always find protection from the sun.

"You two must certainly love to travel," said Jillian.

"I got into event planning by accident. The company phased out the art department where I was a graphic designer. They asked if I wanted to stay on as an event planner. Victor and I were just getting to know each

146

other, so I said yes."

"I meant that you must love to travel because you and your husband both travel for your jobs and here you are on vacation. I'd want to do the opposite of what I do for a living. But that's just me," the woman hurried to say.

"My husband isn't much for sitting around at home. He likes adventure."

The woman smiled. "And what do you like?"

Ashley didn't know how to answer and felt annoyed that this woman was judging her. After all, they were just sharing a bench. The truth was she didn't know what she wanted anymore. She'd been having disturbing thoughts and her emotions were bouncing up and down like a teeter-totter.

Jillian said, "I'm home with the kids all day, so I like a change of scenery. Only with three kids, it's usually more effort than it's worth, if you know what I mean."

"I can imagine." Ashley continued to draw. Jacob whooped and dunked his sister.

"In fact, we're heading back to the Bay Area in the morning. My husband loved camping here as a kid with his dad. We thought it would be fun, but it's too damn hot."

Ashley winced and hugged her stomach.

"Are you okay?"

"Cramps." From her online research she figured it was a normal part of pregnancy. She hadn't gone to a doctor yet. The pain in her stomach reminded her she'd promised herself she would tell Victor before they headed back to Sacramento.

Her drawing captured Jacob's look of devilish delight as he splashed a wave of water at his sister. She usually kept her drawings, but this time she gave it to Jillian. She'd soon be drawing pictures of her own child.

"You're truly gifted," said Jillian. "Thank you."

That afternoon Victor prepared for Zabriskie Point. He pulled on his hiking shorts with the extra pockets.

Ashley glanced out the window. "Wouldn't a morning hike be a better idea? You could go tomorrow."

"You're the one who can't handle the sun, remember? No need to worry about me."

Ashley bit her fingernail. "I wanted to tell you something."

"You sick? You're paler than usual."

This was her moment. She blurted it out. "Vic, I'm pretty sure I'm pregnant." She held her breath, hoping he wouldn't get angry.

"Impossible. You're on the pill. It's just your imagination." He shoved his feet into hiking boots.

"What if it's not just my imagination?" Her heart thumped unnaturally.

"You can have it taken care of."

He could have been discussing having a wart removed. The blood rushed through her veins and she wanted to scream. Instead she whispered, "What if I don't want to have it taken care of? What if I want to have the baby?"

He pulled his shirt over his head, slowly smoothing it over his stomach muscles. "That's ridiculous." He checked out his profile in the mirror. "You should take a nap while I'm hiking. Rest up for our big evening."

He said it with condescending emphasis on the word big. They'd argued when she'd said she wanted to drive to a ghost town twenty-five miles away to see an aging dancer. The dancer had moved to the desert years ago from back East and bought an old opera house where she still performed a couple of nights a week. The dancer was also an artist, and the story was that many nights no one came to see her, so she had painted a mural of theatre-goers in fancy gowns and tuxedos on the back wall—ensuring that she would always have an audience. Ashley loved that story.

Victor didn't like it when Ashley wanted to do "artsy-fartsy" things. He'd said he didn't want to go, but she intended to go anyway. She rarely stood up to him—she'd learned early in their marriage that it was a waste of time because he always wore her down—but she wanted to see the opera house. Of course, if he later changed his mind and went, he'd be irritable and impatient all evening, ruining it for her.

He gathered his hat and pack for the hike, oblivious to the turmoil inside her.

Her voice trembled. "I want to talk about this baby, Victor."

He dropped his pack on the kitchenette table. "Bad timing, Ash, I've planned this hike for a month. You don't want me to miss it, do you?"

She wanted to explode. What was another stupid hike compared to a life growing inside her? She reached into a kitchen drawer and grabbed a cork screw. She wanted to plunge it into his heart. A twist and a yank, his heart popping out, skewered. Maybe then he'd understand how she felt.

He bent to tie his boot laces, "Ash, where's my water bottle?"

She whirled, grabbed his bottle from the refrigerator, poked it with the cork screw, and jammed the bottle in his pack. Then she stood like a statue, shaking with rage.

Laces tied, Victor straightened and stretched his biceps. He pointed at the cork screw in her hand. "Good idea. Have a glass of wine. It'll help you relax."

He reached over and snagged the pack from the counter. "Let's do this."

She pulled the car over to drop him off at Golden Canyon to begin his hike, her emotions still so raw she couldn't speak. He threw his pack over his shoulder.

"Don't forget to meet me in two hours at the gulch on the other side of Zabriskie Point." He kissed her, did a few leg stretches and headed up the trail.

Ashley paced in the hotel room for an hour, thinking about the Swedish man who died, the dull ache in her groin never subsiding.

When it was time to meet Victor, she drove to the spot and parked, expecting him to be waiting. She looked into the distance. She tried his cell phone, but there was no signal. Running the air conditioner intermittently to keep from roasting, she picked up a few brochures from the back seat and settled down to wait.

One of the brochures mentioned a workshop presented by one of the rangers—100 ways to die in Death Valley. A chill ran up her spine.

She waited an hour, more agitated every second that passed. If she notified the ranger station and Victor was simply a little late, he'd be furious that she didn't trust his ability. Still, she worried.

Victor was strong and healthy. She'd been angry earlier, but her small act couldn't have harmed him. She didn't mean it. She'd read about hormone surges in pregnant women causing irrational emotions. Maybe his lateness wasn't because of that jab to the water bottle. What if he'd fallen into one of those ravines and couldn't get out?

Too restless to sit any longer, she stepped out of the air-conditioned car. The heat beat against her and radiated up from the ground into her legs. She reached back in for her water bottle, but had forgotten it at the hotel. She'd only walk as far as the bend. If she couldn't see him, she'd go for help.

She walked along a gulch through odd rock formations like long fingers reaching toward her. Her shoes crunching through the loose shale and rock sounded like shattered glass. No birds flew overhead. Even the lizards were burrowed safely away from the sun's glare.

The silence pressed down on her. She'd never experienced anything as desolate as this place. The only smell was her skin baking under its layer of sun block.

Ashley looked back but couldn't see the car. Remorse flooded her heart at the thought of the Swedish woman waiting for a husband who never came. It would take too long to retrace her steps to the car and drive to the hotel for help. She kept walking.

The path angled off in different directions. There were two trails where before she'd only noticed one. From reading about the area, she'd learned that flash floods during the spring radically changed the landscape, cutting new gulches and canyons into the terrain. To be safe, she made small towers of rocks at regular intervals to find her way back once she'd found him.

Her skin was slick with sweat and her scalp burned under her short hair. She pulled off her tank top and draped it over her head. No one would see her in her bra in this incinerator. She'd bought the tank top at the hotel gift shop. The graphic cartoon of a skeleton hiker with oversized hiking boots and the saying, "Hike or Die!" had seemed funny at the time.

The gulch forked again, and she didn't know which way to go, so she picked a direction and marked it with a tower.

"Victor!" Her voice came out in a croak. She scanned the area for a tree to shelter her, but there were no trees.

Several borax mine entrances dotted a rise above the gulch. The brochure had said they were dangerous and tourists should stay out. Her mouth was crusty, her head throbbed, and the pain in her stomach intensified with each step. Relentless sun bounced off the rocks and pierced her eyes, even with sunglasses. She wanted to climb into one of those dark caverns for a few minutes of respite from the scorching sun, but she had to go on. She stumbled forward, stopping only to build another rock tower. How many had she done? Ten? Fifteen?

She imagined walking in the cool morning fog at home or in a gentle rain, but she only felt more desperate for water. Another row of mines dotted the ridge ahead. Something appeared to be sticking out of one of the entrances. She wiped the sweat from her eyes, but shimmering halos surrounded everything. Slipping on shale, she climbed toward the mine to get a closer view. It was a human leg. She scrambled to the entrance and peered into the darkness.

Eyes closed, her husband lay panting. She threw herself down next to him. "Victor, wake up!"

His eyes fluttered and closed again. A cramp worse than the others doubled her over. She screamed and lost consciousness.

When Ashley awoke that night and learned they'd been airlifted to the Las Vegas hospital hours earlier, she asked who'd saved them.

Ranger Mike came forward from across the hospital room. Dried blood stained his khaki shirt and shorts. "I wanted to see how you were doing before heading back."

Ashley struggled to form words with her cracked and swollen lips. "How did you find us in the mine?"

"Your white BMW hadn't moved all afternoon so I checked with the hotel to see if anyone was missing. They said you were the owners and you'd been out about five hours." He twirled his hat. "That's a long time to be in the desert. I walked up the ravine until I saw the rock towers."

"I did that so I could find my way back."

Victor spoke from his bed next to her. "I got turned around on one of those gulches and kept going in circles. My water bottle leaked. The water was gone in the first half hour. I couldn't get a signal on my cell to call for help." He smiled at Ashley. "I'd be dead if you hadn't come for me."

She looked at her blistered hands, an angry red against the white sheets. "Ranger Mike saved us."

A nurse said the doctor needed to speak to them. She ushered Ranger Mike from the room and the doctor came in holding a clipboard like a shield in front of her. "I'm so sorry. I have bad news."

Victor looked uncomprehending. "We're both alive. What could be wrong?"

Ashley's heart thumped in her chest. The doctor cleared her throat, "I'm afraid you lost the baby."

An anguished cry exploded from Ashley. "No!"

Victor's eyebrows shot up. "You really were pregnant?"

On the drive back to Sacramento the next morning, Victor kept his eyes on the road. "We were almost a repeat of the story about the couple from Sweden."

She licked her charred lips and stared ahead.

He darted a look at her. "You couldn't stop crying when you found out about the miscarriage."

"About my baby," she muttered.

"You don't want a baby." He showed his salesman's smile. "We agreed that wouldn't work with our lifestyle."

She looked away. "I guess not."

He patted the top of her head. "That's right. We have each other. You know you're my baby."

He squeezed her sunburned hand on the seat next to him. "Seriously, Ash, I promise we'll go anywhere you like on our next vacation."

Three months later, they sat in the family room after dinner. Victor watched his favorite football team from his black leather recliner.

Seated in her chintz chair on the other side of the fireplace, Ashley looked up from her laptop. "Remember when you said I could pick the next trip?" Her arms circled the slight rise in her stomach.

He flipped through the channels. "No way. You'd pick an art gallery tour."

"Actually, I've been researching a challenging hiking trail in China, but it's probably too dangerous for you."

He put the recliner in its upright position. "You're joking, right? Nothing's too dangerous for me. Book it."

The deadly Mt. Huashan trail in China had claimed many lives with its sheer drops and treacherous terrain. Ashley pondered the possibilities as she made the arrangements—a frayed shoelace, a slippery winter climb, or an undetectable substance drunk just before hiking that could cause a problem with equilibrium.

EPILOGUE

Chloe attempts to fit a yellow plastic doughnut onto a green one. She aims, her tiny hands shoot forward, but she misses the target and wails. Ashley sets aside her pad and colored pencils, drops to the floor and guides her daughter's hand to the top of the plastic pyramid. Chloe squeals and a triumphant grin replaces her tears.

It's a good lesson. Try, try again.

Ashley glances at the photo of Victor above the fireplace with the giant marlin. It's unfortunate that he never saw his daughter. She has fair skin, strawberry curls and blue eyes. She will freckle.

LINDA TOWNSDIN lives in Carmichael, CA near the American River where she is inspired daily on her walks and bike rides. Until recently, she was senior editor-writer for a criminal justice organization. That background has been helpful in plotting her Spirit Lake mysteries. Two are ready for publication, and the third in the series is nearly finished. She's a member of Sisters in Crime, She Writes, Mystery Must Advertise, and Amherst Writers & Authors which has published three of her short stories in its anthologies. Her blog, "A Writer's Journey," was recently highlighted on Freshly Pressed: Visit her at www.LindaTownsdin.wordpress.com

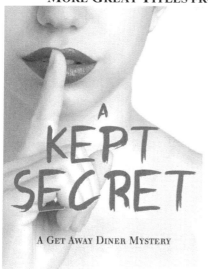

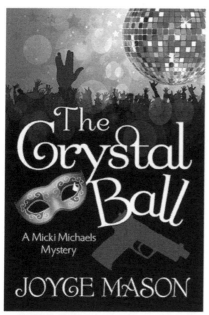

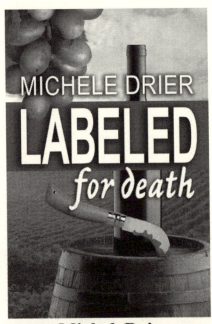
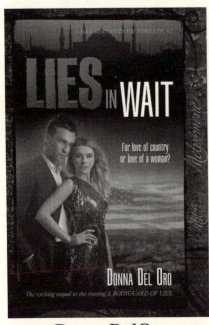
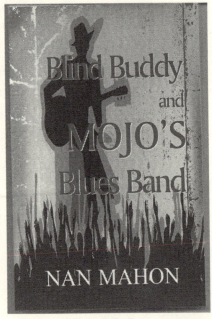

FallenAngelsBookClub.com

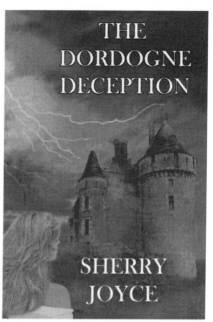

www.SherryJoyce.com

www.PatMyst.com

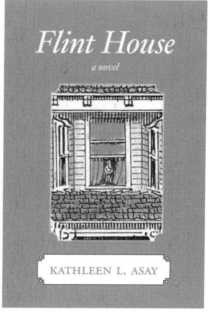

www.KathleenLAsay.com

Made in the USA
San Bernardino, CA
29 October 2013